AFTER REV. TREMMEL IS KILLED, MASON AND HIS TROUPE OF HIGH SCHOOL SENIORS UNRAVEL A BEVY OF TITILLATING SECRETS.

In a small southern town during the 1970s, Mason and his teen age friends have a special relationship with the young, hip, cool, suave, Rev. Tremmel, pastor of the Mt. Sinai Baptist Church. The young men admire Rev. Tremmel and his beautiful, sophisticated wife, Ms. Sonya. However, Mason discovers that Rev. Tremmel is not what he appears to be. His mesmerizing façade eventually unravels, revealing that Rev. Tremmel is deeply intertwined with residents of the town in ways Mason could have never imagined. Other people eventually find out who and what Rev. Tremmel really is, and someone kills him. Mason works on his own to find who did it.

"Burgh paints an intimate portrait of life in small town Georgia, with plot twists and turns that keep the book fresh and engaging. The coming-of-age story, with a healthy dose of humor, extremely interesting characters and an ever growing undercurrent of menace, makes for a real page-turner. I can't remember the last time I read an entire novel in one sitting! I especially enjoyed the young adult characters as they bonded, struggled and overcame the challenges they faced, both interpersonal and from situations forced upon them. Highly recommended reading!" —*Mr. Kevin Kolb, Composer, Musician, IT Director, GPM Southeast, LLC* .

Also by Theodore W. Burgh

Listening to the Artifacts

Are You Going to Eat That?

Sock Monsters

Is God Funky or What? (Expected 2018)

YES, I KILLED REV. TREMMEL
Theodore W. Burgh

Moonshine Cove Publishing, LLC
Abbeville, South Carolina U.S.A.

This book is a work of fiction. Names, characters, places and incidents are products of the author's imagination or are used fictitiously. Any resemblance to actual events, locales or persons, living or dead, is entirely coincidental.

ISBN: 978-1-945181-139
Library of Congress PCN: 2017907114
Copyright 2017 by Theodore W. Burgh

All rights reserved. No part of this book may be reproduced in whole or in part without written permission from the publisher except by reviewers who may quote brief excerpts in connection with a review in a newspaper, magazine or electronic publication; nor may any part of this book be reproduced, stored in a retrieval system or transmitted in any form or by any means electronic, mechanical, photocopying, recording or any other means, without written permission from the publisher.

Front cover image by Andy Bilinski; cover and interior design by Moonshine Cove staff.

ABOUT THE AUTHOR

"Do you sleep?" is a question Burgh hears often. Because he's constantly involved in some kind of creative endeavor — music, art, and writing — many inquire about how he is able to do all that he does. Burgh enjoys exploring different ways to express himself. In particular, he loves combining music to enhance storytelling. His tales often inspire compositions that provide depth and insightful dimensions to a story's characters and various actions that take place. Burgh is an archaeologist and university professor. His research and excavations have taken him to Brazil, Israel, Jordan, and Sicily, as well as other places around the world. Mentoring youth and teaching music keeps him active in the local community. He and his wife Ann enjoy their lives in Wilmington, NC. They have a beautiful daughter and three handsome grandsons. Burgh is also very active in composing and performing music.

More about Dr. Burgh is available at his web page, teddyburgh.com and at his University of North Carolina Wilmington faculty web page, http://uncw.edu/par/faculty/faculty-burgh.html.

To my wife Ann — my ride or die no matter what. I love you.

Acknowledgment

There are many who contributed to the development of this work, and I am truly grateful to each of them. Because the list is long, I often hesitate naming people because inevitably someone is mistakenly omitted. However, I must thank my wife Ann for her undying support and understanding. When I'm locked away in my special place trying to create, you allow me to be without protest. I also appreciate your patience and candidness when reading my thoughts and ideas. Special gratitude also goes to my editor and an incredible human being, Sarah Bode. Your insightful editing skills and belief in my writing inspired me to bring Tremmel to fruition.

Yes, I Killed Rev Tremmel

CHAPTER ONE

"You so flickted, Mason Alexander." Phaedra says. "You got the biggest feet I ever seen."

The rest of the neighborhood brood, probably about twelve or so teenagers, cackle at Phaedra's barbs. I know my mind, vocabulary, and tongue are quick enough to take my anger and embarrassment out on any of them. And that I could completely annihilate her. But what would be the point? It would only generate more tension to deal with, and I already had enough.

Besides, she says this nearly every time she sees me. There's nothing I can do about being "flickted." Hey, I'm fifteen. Soon, but not soon enough, to be sixteen. Everything on me is goofy and "flickted." Little does she realize that I see "flickted" every day when I look in the mirror. My wide pug African nose. My slightly pimpled skin face. My burgeoning but slightly lopsided teeny weenie Afro. My small patch of twelve short, wild, virgin whiskers peeking from my cleft chin. And it seems that no matter what lotion I use, I'm cursed to wear this ashy, walnut-colored skin.

It's all goofy and "flickted" to me, and I really don't need her or anyone else stating the obvious. The embarrassment Phaedra initiated is magnified because of all the other teenagers standing around. I don't know what it is about teenagers, but we take such pride in seeing others humiliated but go to great lengths to avoid it happening to us.

"Flickted." I still haven't found that word in the dictionary. But one can guess what it means merely by how it sounds. I guess it's some twisted derivative or butchered cognate from the term "afflicted." Nevertheless, this stinging, concocted epithet truly expressed its implied definition of "not normal" as it rolled off Phaedra's scorching tongue and pierced my fragile fifteen-year old psyche.

After digesting Phaedra's habitual verbal berating, the time has come for me to depart from our neighborhood teenage group. The streetlights, the ubiquitous neighborhood alarm clock, are coming on signaling the end of another day in July. Another day of freeze-tag, hide and seek, softball, and other contests is done.

It's about 8:30 p.m. The sun stays with us a long time in the summer in the South, especially in Grimmel, Georgia.

Even though we've been playing games all day and the streetlights have given their signal, some of the guys make an impromptu executive decision to try to get in a quick game of basketball before it gets too dark.

Count me in.

Yep, the boys — Marshall, Mitchell, Dep, Link, and I — should be able to play a quick round of 21 before the absence of light shuts us down.

We decide to head over to Craven Park. They have the best rims and new nets — as of last Friday. It's about a 10-12 minute bike ride. Marshall grabs his ball, throws it under his arm, and we make our way.

The park is right on the edge of the line that divides the black and white sides of town. It's an unspoken rule, but the park is "common ground." We play ball there with any and everybody all the time.

Being black and living in Grimmel in the '70s is no easy feat when it comes to dealing with some white folks. Countless times we've had ignorant whites threaten us with bodily harm, throw eggs at us, or try to run us off the road when we're riding our bikes or walking. I've been targeted to be in earshot of tasteless caustic racial humor, set up for embarrassment in the classroom, and endured other torturing incidents.

It's tough to deal with, but it's a part of life where we live.

We ride at a pretty good clip, trying to conserve as much daylight as we can. All the while, we drone about mundane nonsense and brag about who was going to do what to whom on the court.

"I'm gon' dunk on all y'all." Marshall boasts.

"You ought to, with them long arms of yours. But you won't." Dep responds.

"That's all right," I say. "I'm gon' light all y'all up from the top of the key — with my left hand."

Our red, yellow, green, black, and orange ten speeds make a colorful palette as our group races the sun down the far side of the roadway.

We hear an engine roar a good distance behind us, and it gets louder by the second. The sound increases and tells us a pickup truck is coming up fast. We're on a wide two-lane road with plenty of room to pass us, but the truck stays on our side.

Here we go again. We prepare ourselves.

The powder blue '65 Chevy pickup and its occupants mean no good. The vehicle gets closer and slows. Its passenger side is closest to us. We pedal faster.

A "hey niggers." attacks our ears. Followed by a large wad of spit, splattering on the ground just behind Marshall's rear tire.

Having had similar experiences, we respond quickly with learned and creative expletives and flying middle fingers.

"Stupid Peckawood."

"Honky ass bitch."

"Dickless cracker."

As the truck moves past us, Mitchell manages to jump off his bike and launch a few rocks. One lands in the truck's bed.

They speed up, but we see that the passenger is a young guy, probably about our age. His long blond hair blown by the gentle breeze, and the truck's acceleration partially covers his face. He wears sunglasses. But he still looks familiar.

As Marshall pedals a little harder, he careens his neck forward and to the right to get a better look at the passenger.

"That's BJ." he yells.

Billy Guthrie, Jr. Our schoolmate, the son of a known Grimmel racist, obviously hasn't fallen far from the tree.

The truck stops at the light. We try to catch up with them, but the cowards hit the gas as soon as the light changes, screeching and swerving down the road. They punctuate their terrorist act by flinging a half-filled beer can out of the driver's window. The contents spill when it smacks the ground, sending the smell of alcohol back to us.

I'm not sure how given the quickness with which everything happens, but Link got the tag number.

This isn't the first time we've been called "niggers," but the spitting from that punk sent us over the edge. We want to do something about it. After a quick meeting and some unfounded reasoning, we decide to tell Rev. Tremmel.

We blaze a trail for Mt. Sinai Baptist.

We burn up the driveway, skid around the curve to the back of the fellowship hall where the pastor's study is. The light is on in his office.

All five of us run inside. Link throws Rev. Tremmel's office door open and we follow him inside, huffing, puffing, sweating, and trying to gather ourselves.

Rev. Dexter Tremmel is sitting in his large brown leather chair behind his desk. His back faces us. The chair spins around and stops. He looks at us over the top of the large book he's reading.

"What can I do for you guys?" he asks.

Everyone spits bits and pieces at him, trying to explain what happened. He's locked in — catching and listening to every word. Not saying anything.

Rev. Tremmel's the consummate teacher. He's always pointing out some life lesson or giving us insight about something that's right in our faces. One thing he constantly talks to us about is being proud of who we are as Black people. Especially given the time and place we live in.

The man is very passionate and sensitive about the mistreatment of anyone, and even more so for those blessed with an ebony hue. He told us to be sure that we let him know if we had any problems with anyone or anything dealing with race.

Here we are.

Once we stop pelting him with our versions of what happened, he reacts just as we thought. Rev. Tremmel hits the roof.

"So they want to call you that? And they want to spit on you? Okay. We'll see about that.

"Hold on a second gentlemen. I need to make a quick phone call, and we'll get on this right now."

Rev. Tremmel dials seven digits on his black rotary phone. "Hey baby. Yes, I know. Look, I'm going to be a little late. Something's come up with a few of the boys. You know Mason, Dep, and those guys. I think they're all right, but I need to handle this now. I'll be there soon. Bye now."

Tremmel hangs up the receiver and turns back to us.

"Mrs. Tremmel worries about me. Have to let her know what's going on. You fellas understand, right?"

We nod, not sure if we understand or not. But it's Rev. Tremmel.

After making sure we're okay, Rev. Tremmel gets our little country police department on the phone and has them run a check on the license plate.

"Captain Butterfield, please."

He turns to us and says, "We'll get to the bottom of this."

We nod confidently, knowing that we have an advocate.

Rev. Tremmel says sternly into the receiver, "Captain Butterfield, Rev. Tremmel here. I'm fine. Hey, check this tag number for me and tell me who it's registered to. And hurry up."

Damn. He's talking to Captain Butterfield like that? Rev. Tremmel has some juice.

In a couple of minutes Captain Butterfield tells him that the truck is registered to Billy Guthrie, Sr.

We go to school with BJ — Billy Guthrie, Jr.

Marshall was right. BJ was the spitter and insulter.

BJ's an enormous country-fed white boy; and his father, who's a redneck big wig in town, is also a jerk. They say and do whatever they please. I'm not sure why, but everyone seems to be scared of both of them — including us. BJ's bullied us a bunch of times before, and we didn't do anything about it.

Rev. Tremmel calms us down and assures us that everything's going fine. "Don't worry about anything guys. The main concern for me is that all of you all are okay. Don't pay those ignorant fools any attention. God has a way of dealing with folks like that."

We'd like to help God deal with them, I think.

His phone rings. "Excuse me guys, I need to get this."

Tremmel picks up the phone again, "Hello? What's happening my man? You got it? Good. Look, I'll meet — "

Rev. Tremmel covers the receiver with his chest and speaks to us, "Okay guys. I'll see you Sunday morning, right?"

"Right," we say in unison.

"Don't worry about anything," he assures us.

He turns his attention back to the person on the phone.

"Okay, I'm back. Some of the young men from my congregation. Good guys."

Rev. Tremmel continues his conversation as we back out of the study. Link's the last one out and closes the door behind him.

"Man. Did you hear how he talked to Captain Butt?" I whisper.

They all nod.

"Rev. Tremmel is a bad dude," Link says.

King, Malcolm, Parks, Abernathy, Bond, Davis, Carmichael and others have worked and continue to work hard for equality and justice, but it often feels like neither has completely arrived in Grimmel.

Being Black in my world also means that you have to have a sixth sense for covert as well as blatant acts of racism, terrorism, speak another language in the presence of whites, and in many ways — know your place. Our encounters with people like BJ are constant reminders.

We pedal home from Mt. Sinai Baptist. No rousing game of 21 for us today. Terrorized yet again.

But we feel good after sharing our story with Rev. Tremmel, seeing his genuine concern, and hearing him put his words in action.

***

It's been a couple of days since the name calling-spitting incident. It's still fresh in our minds, but thanks to Rev. Tremmel we're not dwelling on it.

Today is full of the summer trademark Grimmel thunderstorms. They're dictating and controlling outdoor activities, so we all decide to meet at the skating rink on Curtis Drive. I take my chances and walk the half-mile between storms to the rink. Just as I make my way up the slight incline in the parking lot, Dep runs up to me.

"C'mon. Man you got to see this." he says, grinning.

I pull my skates off my shoulder and trot behind him, the strings of the skates cut into my fist. He stops at the area where the smokers do their thing.

"Look," he says, staring at me but nudging his head slightly to the left. I follow the direction of his pointing. It leads to BJ.

He's looking at the ground, talking to two other white guys and working hard to suck the nicotine from a half-finished cigarette.

When BJ raises his head slightly, I see busted lips, a swollen, crimson and purple right eye that's nearly closed, and an inflated face decorated with black and blue bruises, ornamented with just-starting-to-heal scratches. I nearly gasp out loud.

BJ looks up and sees Dep and me. He gives a quick nod acknowledging our presence and shamelessly goes back to looking at the ground. The other two look at us and look back at BJ. They don't say a word.

Dep snickers.

"Somebody tore off in his ass." he whispers as we walk to the entrance of the rink.

I'm not sure what Rev. Tremmel did, but I know he's responsible for BJ's face. The man's like a mafia don — he speaks and things happen. I hope he doesn't have people whacked.

I don't think we're going to have any more problems with BJ. Of course, all of our racial issues aren't resolved, but I believe I can safely say this one is.

Rev. Tremmel's something else. Everybody loves the man and for good reason.

He tells us all the time, "Grimmel rhymes with Tremmel, so this is where I'm supposed to be."

I'm a little nervous with what happened to BJ, but it feels good to know Rev. Tremmel's looking out us.

When I get home from the skating rink, I tell my father about what happened. Like Rev. Tremmel, he's upset.

"Damn it." my father shouts. He steps off the porch and kicks my sister's red ball hard sending it across the yard.

"Dad, I would've told you sooner, but you weren't home when it happened."

"No it ain't that. It's just a damn shame that in this day and age y'all gotta still deal with junk like this.

"I'm glad you told Tremmel." My father sighs. "At least he got that damn Butterfield off his fat ass and made him do something besides eat."

After some thought, it may have been a good thing that my dad wasn't at home. He's a quiet guy, but I've seen him angry, and it's not pretty. It's scary actually. He might've killed BJ and anyone that was with him if I'd told him what happened instead of Rev. Tremmel.

"You know, I kinda like that Tremmel," my father says, as we walk over to get the ball.

This is big, because he's not into preachers and churches.

"You know, I saw Tremmel the other day up at the drugstore," my father continues. "There was this elderly lady there. I didn't know who she was. She might've been from outta town. But she was in a bad way though. Lookin' rough. Hair all over the place. Face filthy. Didn't have enough money to pay for what she had.

"I was watchin' her real close," he says, squinting his eyes hard, almost as if he was looking at her again.

"'Cause I seen people like that run games. They can have you thinkin' one thing and the next thing you know, they takin' yo' money or callin' the cops on you. I didn't want to get caught up in no mess with her and them folks in the drugstore."

That's my father. He's suspicious of everybody and everything initially. He had a run-in with Captain Butterfield a few years ago that made matters worse. He was leaving the Buy-Lo grocery store one afternoon and saw a lady struggling to put her groceries in her car. He went over and started helping her. She looked at him and screamed at the top of her lungs. Capitan Butterfield was in the parking lot and came over.

"What's going on here ma'am?" Butterfield asked.

The woman told him, "That man tried to steal my groceries."

My father was furious. He had to explain and defend himself for trying to help this woman.

"Look man, I was just trying to help the woman," he said. "Her groceries were falling all over the ground."

"Are you sure weren't tryin' to help yourself to her groceries, boy?" Butterfield said.

"Hell no. And you know I wasn't."

The lady didn't say anything. She never acknowledged that my father was trying to help her. After more unnecessary probing from Butterfield he finally let my father go. But to this day he's very cautious about jumping in to be a Good Samaritan.

"When I could see the old lady was for real," my father says, "I went to go help her, but Tremmel beat me to it. I didn't even see him. He came outta nowhere. Tremmel got her what she needed, paid for her stuff. We both helped her outside. He put her in a cab and said he would meet her at the shelter.

"He's all right. Yep, Tremmel's all right."

My father didn't like the previous pastor of Mt. Sinai at all. I'm too young to remember him, but he made it clear to me that he didn't like him and any other preacher — not even a little.

"That fool was a charlatan. A greedy son of a bitch. Typical jackleg preacher. Full o' shit. Had them people runnin' around like they was crazy, doin' whatever he say.

"He told them, 'Bible say give ten percent of yo' money.' Yeah, it say 'Yo' body's a temple too. He never said anything about that. That fat fool would eat anything that stopped movin', and would screw anything with a hole in it. Why don't folks use their brains and think sometime?"

For him to say something kind about a preacher says a lot about what he thinks about Rev. Tremmel.

Being fifteen — almost sixteen — in rural Georgia is torture. You're too young to drive, and you're too old to do many of the things that the pre-pubescents do. It's adolescent purgatory.

I can't wait until next year. Hell, knowing me, I'll still probably find something else to complain about. But for now, I can hardly wait. I've just got to make it through the summer.

It's hard to believe it's mid-August already. We've spent another hot, humid day running, jumping, eating, and just being. The sun's almost to bed, and we find ourselves running through the field near my house gently cupping our hands together around slow moving lightening bugs. They're lovely insects with a unique incandescent talent, but they leave a funky smell on your hands.

We catch lightening bugs and jail them in glass jars, watching their bottoms blink on and off until they extinguish and die. The scent they leave behind reminds me of the memories we create as we squeeze every ounce of enjoyment from the fleeting freedom of summer.

Time to head home for the night. There should be something good on TV, but more than likely, part of the neighborhood clan — probably the guys — will make their way to my porch to kill off some more muggy summer hours with meaningless, but "important" conversation — frivolous diatribes and incredible accounts of skillful lying.

Just as I predicted, here come the fellas. The motley bunch makes their way to our long rectangular cement front porch. The pungent smell of hard-earned-teenaged funk much like the lightening bugs, mixes with the humid night air. It arrives a few seconds before they do.

The five of us make comfortable spots along the edge of the porch and in some of the mismatched chairs. Marshall, the tallest of the bunch, plants his lanky six feet, four-inch frame on a cracking cedar bench. Mitchell, the master of double-talk and fabrication, perches himself precariously on the arm of a peeling brown wicker chair. Link sits a few feet from Dep on the edge of the porch. And I sit on the spotty lawn in front of them.

The lying commences immediately — Mitchell spread-ing the first layer.

"Man, I wish we could get out of Georgia," he says in his high-pitched voice. "Ain't nothing going on here. Ain't nothin' to do, no girls, no nothing," he says.

You can tell from our pseudo-hatred of the state that we hadn't traveled very much. Most of us are lucky if we've made it out of the state by the time we reach our teens. Some had made the trek up North once or twice, but we knew very little about the rest of the world, aside from living through other folks' travels, pictures from magazines, textbooks, and slanted stories from school or the news.

At some point in every single one of our conversations, it's mandatory for us to talk, well, lie about our favorite subject — girls.

Mitchell continues, "When I get outta school, I'm movin' to Virginia. Y'all remember Angela's cousin 'Nita from Richmond? Man, she was fine. Every girl I seen from Virginia is fine. I'm moving to Virginia soon as I get out."

"I don't know about Virginia," Link says. "I think I'm goin' back to New York. Them Rican sisters is fine. That long black hair and brown skin. Man, I don't know what they be sayin,' but it sound good to me."

His words brought to mind a few of the attractive Puerto Rican sisters that were attending our high school.

"Negro, please," Dep says. "You was barely a year old when y'all got here from New York. You ain't know yo' name, much less somethin' bout some Rican girls. You outta stop lyin' talkin' bout you goin' back to New York. You don't know nothin' bout no New York."

Dep, the smoothest cat in our ensemble, never misses an opportunity to challenge Link's ephemeral connections with New York.

All of us in our little ragamuffin gang are pretty tight with each other, but Dep and Link have a strange relationship. The two of them can't get along with each for very long. For starters, they're insanely jealous of each other, and a bit of this envy is connected to the young men's differing skin colors.

In Grimmel, being light-skinned, "high yella" or "red," is worn and perceived by a lot of people as a badge of honor and creates a place of privilege for some in society.

You can look like the bottom of a combat boot trampled through cow manure, but if you're light, you're considered "fine" and have advantages others can't obtain. Let me break this down a little more. If you have curly hair and light skin, you belong to an even more elite social class. It's unbelievable how many categories people make based on these relatively uncontrollable physical features. I don't understand why, but they're there. They're for real.

Dep wears these badges proudly, and on occasion, rubs them in our darker hued faces and through our kinky hair.

Link, on the other hand, bears physically what some might call the mark of Cain. The biblical story of Cain and Abel says that although Cain killed his brother, God gave him a mark so that no one should harm him. In Link's case, it's a mark that can keep people away, but also bring a pain felt deep in one's spirit. His skin is extremely dark and flawless. It's smooth like glass and supple. Link couldn't have a pimple if he wanted one. But, his deep chocolate, unblemished complexion, slightly coarse, thick jet-black hair and straight pearly white teeth are no match for the power of the light skin in our neck of the woods.

I still hear members of Grimmel's black community, particularly the older sisters at church, refer to Link as "that blue-black child" or "Mandingo black, but clean." Others describe him with pejorative phrases — "he ain't nobody's pretty child." They even evoke the drudges of oppressive slave plantation life with the slanderous monikers "Shine" or "Sambo."

Even though these are hideous degrading epithets spouted by the ignorant, there's no mistaking that Link isn't considered to be anywhere close to the elite, special, more "acceptable" class of the lighter hue.

Link's grandmother, Mrs. Flora Potts, has taken care of him from the beginning. His mother died giving birth to him in New York, and Mr. and Mrs. Potts brought him here shortly afterwards. Mr. Potts passed on a few years ago from a heart attack. When Link was a toddler, his father died under strange circumstances. The story is that he was killed supposedly in some freak accident while traveling in Europe. Link's never really bought that story, but that's the only one he knows. Even though Link didn't know his father, I can tell from some of our conversations that Mrs. Potts is still trying to fill the void his mother but especially his father's death left.

Mrs. Potts has a dark mocha complexion and understands the weight Link carries. When she sees that someone is even thinking about uttering a derogatory comment about her baby, Mrs. Potts is happy to tell them where to go and how to get there. That lady loves Link to the hilt.

He acts like he's embarrassed sometimes because of her chutzpah, but he loves the confidence and protection that she gives him.

Although he never verbalizes it, Link hates that people disqualify or stigmatize him because of his skin color. He resents the fact that anyone views his deep chocolate shade as a mark of shame or affliction, or that he's considered less than everyone else or not so smart as others. But he bears his imputed societal cross rather well.

The five of us are all close, but I know that Link likes talking to me about different things before he would with some of the other guys. I guess it's because I try not to judge. It's not that I'm trying to be like Jesus or anything like that. Most of the time, I don't know what to say. So I just listen. He and I've talked many times about the crap he gets about his skin color and other intimate thoughts about his life. He's candid with me. But he knows I won't ever say a word, and I know he'll do the same.

Just last week Link shared an incident with me involving that ornery Mrs. Emma Winston.

"Man, you know what that ol' witch Mrs. Winston said to me when I was trimming her hedges last week?"

"What?"

"'Boy you sho' is black. Whew. I didn't realize how black you was. How you get so dark? Don't you stay out here in that sun too long. You can't afford to get no blacker.' And that cow had the nerve to laugh as she walked off. Ha-ha my ass.

"Mason, it took all I had not to cuss her ol' feeble wrinkled ass out. I'm out here in the hot sun, cuttin' this heifer's grass, trimming her hedges — only cause my grandmother asked me to. And she gon' say some dumb shit like that?

"That's crazy." I say. "Did you say anything back to her?"

"Are you crazy? That cow woulda called my grandmother and then called Rev. Tremmel. You know how she do."

"Yeah, I do."

"And you know Mrs. Winston ain't that light herself. And she ain't little neither. Walkin' around the yard behind me, huffin' and puffin' and sweatin' gravy. Knowin' it was too hot for her big behind to be out there. If she'd passed out, I woulda left her big ass right there on the ground."

I chuckle. Link is letting her have it. I let him go. He needs to get this out.

"Gon' call somebody black. She ain't but two shades away from Shinola herself. Why does she think she can say that shit and get away with it? I tell you why. She's old and uses it to get what she wants and do what she wanna do. She's plays that 'respect your elders' mess. I respect my elders man, but this ol' bat is pushing it.

"You did the right thing, man. You woulda had your grandma and Rev. Tremmel on your case if you said anything."

"You right. But if she didn't know my grandmother and wouldn't run tell Tremmel everything. I'd a lit her ol' ass up."

Even though he was upset with Mrs. Winston, I could see what she said hurt him deep.

I feel for him.

"Hey man," I say. "You heard anything about Cleotis Johnson tippin' around Mrs. Winston's house — at night?"

"What? Get outta here with that."

"I heard my mother gossipin' on the phone the other day, and she said something about it. Supposedly somebody saw him over at her place."

"That's news to me. Wait. Now that I think about it, I heard somebody say something like that, but I didn't pay attention to it."

As we get the mental picture of Mr. Johnson and Mrs. Winston being intimate, we both crack up at the thought.

"That's nasty."

"Yep. Snuff-dippin' Cleotis Johnson and fat ass, thick ankles Emma Winston? Yuk."

"We gotta stop," Link says, laughing and holding up his hands in submission. "I can't take anymore. I got that image stuck in my head."

"Me too." I wipe the tears from my cheeks.

"I can't believe that witch called me 'black' " Links says.

A little revenge was in order though for Mrs. Winston's mistreatment of Link. A few days later Link and I made a special trip to her house. We had a lovely time pissing on the old woman's prize rose bushes.

Just a little redemption for my man.

One of the reasons Link and Dep don't always get along besides the color thing is they're so much alike and both always want to be the center of attention. They try to outdo each other in everything. It's a constant spitting contest between them. One of them always has to win. They compete against each other directly or indirectly in every game and sport we play. At Hide and Go Get It (a game like Hide and Seek but we try to "hide" with a girl so we can try to make out), they argue over who hides the best. They both lose all the time at board games, but they bicker over who loses the worst.

Many would consider our spontaneous neighborhood track meets absurd, but the ancient Greeks would be proud of the competitive spirit.

For instance, if Link or Dep loses a foot race to the other, they have to have a rematch immediately. It's as if they lay awake at night thinking of ways to get the best of each other. When we play baseball, football, or basketball, they have to play on opposite teams. When we got part time jobs and started earning a little cash for clothes and incidentals, Link and Dep started arguing over who's the best dresser, who has the best kept hair, and of course they perpetually competed for ladies' accolades and attention.

Ironically, although the two fight like cats and dogs, there's an unwritten rule that no one is allowed to say anything negative about either of them or that person will have a bad day. It isn't obvious initially, but there's some unique, deep almost blood brother-like bond between them. I can't quite put my finger on it.

The lying-fest finally begins to wind down. Each of us has presented slivers of our unique imaginations, and Mitchell has come full circle back to the subject of girls. Sadly, his fables are getting sickening and a bit offensive. He lies in graphic detail about the number of women he's bedded.

Of course we know he's slinging crap, but it's something about the way the brother can spin lies that keeps us listening and entertained.

But in the list of girls he claims to have kissed, felt up, or "got some from," he lets the wrong name slip off his tongue. I thought he did it on purpose, but how could he know how I feel?

Why did he have to say he touched Rhonda?

I've had a crush on this girl since the third grade. I still remember the first time I saw her. She was helping a teacher clear off one of the cafeteria tables. That caramel skin — her hair color is on the cusp or where yellow and brown meet. Those thick yellow yarn ribbons adorning her two dangling, curly dark brown ponytails. The matching yellow culottes, pea green knee-high socks, and red sneakers sent me over the edge.

We've been in school together for about 8 years, and in all that time, I think we've exchanged 12 meaningless words and a few pleasantries. That's my fault. I can't help it. My tongue melts when she comes within 10 feet of me. Man, she's it.

And here I sit fuming, but listening quietly to Mitchell commit blasphemy about sleeping with "my girl," well even if she didn't know she was mine.

Link's the only one that knows I have a thing for Rhonda, but he doesn't say a word. He slides me a concealed look and half-grin as Mitchell weaves his tale.

The oft-quiet Marshall finally speaks up and challenges him on his bullshit.

"Man you ain't slept with no Rhonda or nobody else. Matter of fact, you don't even know what poontang smell like."

We fall over each other. I thought Dep was going to choke. He couldn't catch his breath. He finally lets out a scream followed by a cackle. When Link falls down, we know whatever happened or what was said was funny, and this time he goes down like a ton of bricks. The boy is lying on the porch, his body convulsing with laughter.

I want to thank Marshall for salvaging the dignity of my girl since I didn't have the courage to.

We have to be careful though. Mitchell and Marshall are slow to anger, but they have horrible tempers. And when angry, they're calculating and vindictive. We all look out for each other, but these two are downright frightening. Let's just say, I'm glad they're my friends.

Last summer we were at Eastern Park hanging out and a cat from Rose Grove pushed Dep hard from behind, causing him to stumble and nearly fall. He mumbled something about us not being from around there and needed to go.

"I'm cool," Dep said. "Don't worry about it. He's just bein' stupid. Let's go."

We remained calm, kept to ourselves. But this guy kept yapping. We stayed a little while longer, checked out the girls playing softball and finally decided to leave.

The clown started up again. We kept walking.

I remember saying, "Hey, Dep, y'all wanna grab some —"

All of a sudden we heard a smack and breaking glass. When we turned around, we saw that Marshall had hit the trash-talker upside the head with a soda bottle and kicked him in the nuts. The guy went down in a heap. Bleeding cuts and slivers of glass filled his face. Mitchell kicked him over and over hard in the back — *thunk. thunk. thunk.* Dust clouds formed from Mitchell's flying feet. The poor guy moaned like a sick dog, grabbing at his face and groin. He tried to cover his back from Mitchell's feet.

Marshall stood over him holding the rest of the broken bottle screaming, "I can't hear you man? What you say? Say somethin' else. You wanna push somebody? Push me."

The trash-talker's boys ran leaving their buddy lying on the ground, bleeding, crying, humiliated. We grabbed Marshall and Mitchell and took off.

We knew they had tempers, but where did this extreme violence come from?

"I had enough of that fool," Marshall said.

"Me too," said Mitchell. "When he pushed Dep, I tried to let it go, but he wouldn't shut up. When I saw Marshall smack 'em, I wanted to help him finish the job."

Still waters really do run deep.

Those are my boys — competitive, violent, thoughtful — I wouldn't trade them for anything.

The clock is striking 1:30 a.m. It's still hot, muggy, sticky, and boring. Buzzing streetlights, crickets, and frogs provide the theme music for the night as the gang of four head off to their respective homes.

Our parents are strict, but they're pretty lenient in letting us stay outside until the early morning hours. They know exactly where we are. We're all in earshot, and our pride and young legs can take each of us home in seconds.

Once everyone leaves, I slip in the house. The entrance empties into our small living room. In the midst of darkness, my father clutches a half-empty can of Pabst Blue Ribbon, stretched out in his recliner. The TV lights dance on his sleeping face.

The rest of the house is serene but hot and humid from the sweltering night heat.

I hear my sisters breathing in harmony, as they pay their nocturnal dues. The outline of their bunk beds creates a silhouette against their opened curtained window.

As I approach my room, I look to my right and through her cracked bedroom door, I see my mother relaxing on her bed. A movie has her attention. Without looking up, she asks, "Is everyone gone home?"

"Yes, ma'am," I reply as I walk into my room — my sanctum of peace. I close the door behind me and collapse on my bed. My mind spins like a roulette wheel briefly stopping to reflect on the memories of another summer day, but it finally settles on Mitchell's lies about Rhonda.

As I revisit the creative lustful tales of his encounters with her, my blood boils all over again. I know he hasn't touched her, but the thought of him even thinking about it is devastating.

Why do I like this girl so much? She barely knows I'm alive. But there's something I feel for her that paralyzes my mind.

This morning as I prepare to enter the realms of deep sleep, I dial up my fantasies about our first date, our wedding, honeymoon, two children, and brick house with a white picket fence and small dog.

This is what I've seen the rich white folks have on TV, so this is what Rhonda and I should have. Hey, they look happy, and it was better than any Black family — real or on TV — I knew. James and Florida on *Good Times*? I like the show and the way they love each other, but to live like them? Give me a break.

In my mind, I have the power to create the perfect life with the perfect girl.

CHAPTER TWO

The summer's drawing to a close. I could never tell my boys, but I'm ready to go back to school. This is my senior year. Yes, me a senior. I'll only be 16 shortly, but I was able to skip a couple of grades in elementary school thanks to tutoring from my parents, grandmother and aunts.

It's bittersweet in that I get to finish school early, but it's a pain because I'm confined to teenage prison during what are supposed be the pinnacle years of high school. Well, it'll all be over soon. Still, I can hardly believe I'm a senior. I've been in school almost as long as I can remember, and now the end is in sight.

It looks like all of us should graduate, even though I have a feeling that it may come down to the wire and some grace and mercy for Mitchell and Marshall. These two and a lot of other folks around my way have never liked school. For these guys to get out without quitting would be a dream come true for them and their parents.

Wow. What's it going to be like being top dog at Grimmel High School, home of the Lions? Being a part of the group who "rules the halls." Being one who commands respect from underclassmen. Being a person who'll soon reach the upper echelon of high school education. Whatever. What does the school year of 1979-1980 hold?

***

The year begins as any other. Clothes, especially back to school clothes, are always a big deal. Much time and thought goes into the purchase and selection of one's wardrobe, especially for the first day of school.

Students all over Yellowstone County are preparing to step on high school campuses styling new rags bought with summer job earnings and sporting the latest hairstyles.

My little sisters are an unforgiving litmus test when it comes to fashion. They always provide a thorough critique with plenty of feedback — whether I want it or not.

If I hear, "No, Mason. That don't work." That means I've completely missed the mark and shouldn't leave my room, much less the house.

"Boy, you know that don't go together," means they don't like my choice of colors.

I know I'm in good shape and ready to go when one of them says, "You look cute."

Clothes are important. But what I find most intriguing are the new changes in physical appearances. Our nascent attributes are gifts, but if you ask some, at times they're curses from Mother Nature.

There've been some changes among our group of fellas, but we spend so much time together, our eyes often don't catch the alterations.

Several people though, some girls in particular, notice special modifications in Link. I even see my sisters take a second look at him.

You see, we all fooled around with weightlifting in Dep's backyard during the summer. He has just enough poundage and bars to keep us challenged, interested and exhausted. So a few times a week, we'd go over and attempt to demonstrate the effects of our bubbling testosterone, and sculpt our burgeoning bodies.

I remember one day this summer — the third of July as a matter of fact.

Link says, "Let's 'max out' on the bench."

Maxing out always brought comical moments and a little harmless competition — for the most part. Today didn't disappoint.

I'm pretty strong for my size, and my bench press max has been around 180 pounds. That's not bad for someone who barely weighs 130 soaking wet. Today, I pressed 185. I'm getting close to that magic 200.

Marshall wanted to gain upper body strength and add bulk to his lanky frame, but skipped the bench press max out. He did bicep curls and overhead shoulder presses by the fence. He's so long and thin. He flexed intensely after each set. Marshall twisted, pushed and squeezed his biceps as if he was watching himself in a mirror. He examined his thin wiry arms closely for the slightest change.

"The guns are coming." Link yelled.

Marshall stayed focused on the curls and his arms and didn't respond.

After the last set he threw up a front double bicep pose, and a large vein in the middle of his forehead throbbed. His eyeballs looked like they would leap from his skull. It was hard to determine whether he was flexing or having a difficult bowel movement. The grimaces he made were priceless. It took everything for me not to laugh.

Mitchell skipped the bench press too and did sit-ups with his shirt off on an old raggedy blue mat my sister used to use for tumbling. Sweat poured off his face and concave chest. He was doing the sit-ups so fast he was out of breath.

"Slow down man. It's not a sit-up race," Link says. Mitchell's six-pack was developing, but he was still about two short.

As usual, Link and Dep were competing.

"Dep. Dep. Listen man, you can't push up 200." Link says. "I know you got some decent arms and a little chest on you, but you can't do that."

Dep outweighs me by about 15 pounds, and he's pretty strong. Still, 200 pounds is a lot to bench press.

"Shut up, Link. You don't know what you talking about. I can do this. I-I did it the other day over at my cousin's house. Move out the way."

We slapped the 200 on the bar like he wanted. He slid down on the bench under the slightly oxidized metal bar.

Dep inhaled. Exhaled. Inhaled. Exhaled. He grunted and let out a primordial scream. He swung his arms back and forth across his chest a few times to "loosen up."

"Man, come on." Link yelled. "You takin' all day."

Dep finally put his hands on the bar, carefully measured the distance between his hands, grabbed it tightly, took one more inhale, and pushed it off the rack. But the bar came down fast and hard on his chest — *whump*. He kicked and pushed, huffed, and snorted, but it wouldn't move.

"What's the matter man? C'mon. Push it up." Link says.

"Get this thing off me."

"Huh?" He looked down at Dep and smiled.

"Man let's get this thing off him," I say.

I grabbed one end of the bar, Link picked up the other, and we put it back on the rack.

Link doubled over and fell on the ground laughing.

I tried not to. I put my hand over my mouth, but my sniggering oozed over and through my fingers. Finally, I just let it go.

"Y'all wrong man," Dep says.

He rubbed his chest and arms trying to ease the physical pain and expunge the embarrassment.

He scratched his head.

"I threw up 200 with no problem at my cousin's house. Man, y'all sure y'all got the right number of weights on there? You sure y'all didn't put on 250?"

Link and I started laughing again.

"No. No. Don't even try it, Dep," Link says. "We can count. That's 200. You're the one runnin' around like you Arnold Swarz-a-Negro. That's your fault. I said you couldn't do it — at least not yet. Them weights just whupped your butt."

"Y'all make me sick." Dep went over and sat on an oak stump by Mitchell.

It was really tough for Dep because Link's a natural at weight lifting. It's like his mind is super focused on the body parts he works. He doesn't really strain. His movements are fluid and effortless. It's fun to watch him, and he still tries to teach us.

We watched Link press 200 with no problem. Dep walked away disgusted.

Our egos and testosterone pushed us, but most of our working out was indirectly for the eyes of the young ladies.

All of us were going through natural, youthful changes. Phaedra, tongue everlasting, publicly reminds me about my awkward transformation every chance she gets.

Marshall continues to grow straight up. By the end of the summer he's a gangly six foot five and a half. That's amazing to us.

The rest of us filled out a little in the shoulders and arms, but Link's development was ridiculous. While we fought tooth and nail to add some muscle and definition to our spindly arms, Link exploded overnight.

When we meet at the bus stop the morning of the first day of school, it feels like we're seeing him for the first time.

I don't know if it's the clothes he's wearing, his fresh shag haircut or Vaselined shining face, but this was not the same guy we'd hung out with all summer. He's muscular and cut.

Link even stands differently, lots of confidence, self-assurance.

We're all quietly impressed, baffled, slightly jealous, sneaking glances. But we'll never tell him anything like that. He knows it though.

We exchange our obligatory greetings and handshakes as the bus slows to a stop. The initial leg of the end of my high school journey has officially begun.

The first day ride is racked with dualism. Being a senior means I've reached the peak of high school education. I enjoy what I'm learning in high school, but the social life part is for the birds.

I always feel out of place, goofy, or lost. It's like I'm in a race and constantly running two steps behind everybody else. When I think I've caught up, I figure out that they're still way ahead of me.

I don't like the socially constructed high school rituals, traditions, and bogus rites of passage. Who made up this crap?

And the idea that everybody gets picked on in high school doesn't take into account the indescribable and crippling pain that comes along with it. And not everyone gets teased. That's a load of bull.

The bottom line is that I can't wait to graduate.

Maybe if there wasn't so much peer pressure I'd feel differently. But it's too much. You can lose your mind trying to be cool. If you don't wear these shoes — you're not cool. If you're not a part of this crowd — you're not cool. If you don't speak like this — you're not cool. If you're a guy, and you aren't juggling two or three girls, you're not cool.

All of this makes establishing relationships with girls excruciating.

My parents, especially my father, taught me to always be a gentleman and treat women with respect. It's great — in theory. I try to follow those pearls of wisdom, but they hardly ever work in my favor.

I have a reputation for being a nice, quiet guy. The person who coined the phrase, "nice guys finish last" knew what they were talking about. "Bad" boys always get the girls everyone wants. Guys like me are the ones left to console these same girls after the juvenile ignoramuses jilt them time and time again.

I'd be a billionaire if I had a nickel for every time one of those girls told me, "You're such a good friend."

Hearing this is always the kiss of death for any chance at a romantic relationship, and I received death's kiss too many times.

These thoughts occupy my mind as I settle on the sticky dark green vinyl seat.

I look around at all of the people riding this diesel monster to school. There're so many stories, so much energy, so many lives headed to the same place. I still wonder where in the world do I fit in this social maze? But I quickly remind myself that it doesn't really matter. It'll all be over soon.

The bus stops and the door slams opens into the parking lot. I float with the moving herd.

We're here.

My class schedule is a relatively easy one — English, Creative Writing and French. I can finish my final year with a bang. I've heard about senioritis, but it's a disease I can't afford to catch. If it didn't kill me, my father would.

English is one of my favorite subjects. But if a young black man in Grimmel says he likes reading books, he's labeled a punk, gay, or accused of "acting white." I don't get it. I love reading, writing, and art, and I sure as hell ain't white or gay. I just keep my interests to myself.

Ironically, the first class of the day is English.

I see the usual suspects in my college prep class — the rich, "smart," privileged white girls and guys, the neurotic over achievers, and an ultra-light smattering of the same affirmative-action black faces.

But this time, I see a new but familiar one — Rhonda. I knew she was in the more difficult English classes, but we've never been in the same ones. Now, here she is sitting one row to my left and two desks ahead of me. My prayers have finally been answered.

It took long enough.

She's long since graduated from the red sneakers, dangling ponytails, pea-green socks, and culottes.

Rhonda is shapely with that same caramel skin. Dark brown hair graces the zenith of her shoulders. I might be a virgin, but look at that tight apple bottom. I can imagine doin' some things with that.

She's one of those girls that just wakes up fine. But what attracts me even more is her demeanor. She's quiet and reserved, but not introverted. Kind but not sappy. Confident but not arrogant. And it sounds corny, but she's friendly to everyone. I don't know anyone who doesn't like her. All of this is captivating, intriguing, and intimidating. Still, I'm thrilled to see her in my English class. Maybe I'll get up the courage to say something to her today.

I huff into my hand. Whew. My breath is okay.

CHAPTER THREE

My chance with Rhonda comes sooner than I could've imagined.

Our English teacher, Ms. Lockhart, is innovative. As she goes over the syllabus with us, she explains that she's assigning partners we'll work with in discussing and analyzing scheduled readings, leading certain classes, and a yearlong research project.

My heart begins to race, but I'm not sure why.

First, I'm absolutely petrified at the thought of leading the class in anything, and second, who in the world will be my partner? I slyly look around the room and begin a process of elimination.

Please don't let it be funky breath Chris. That boy's halitosis is putrid and can gag a maggot. And he's so damn lazy. Deal with bad breath and laziness all year? Please don't do that to me, Ms. Lockhart.

Oh no, not Long Lip Lucy either. I bet she puts the people in her dreams to sleep because she talks so much.

I quickly pray for it not to be that simpleton Johnny. This clown is as dependable as the weather. I'll end up doing everything myself if she sticks me with that fool.

And please don't put me with dumb ass Dwayne. The boy will argue with God about the color of the sky.

Steven or Michelle. Yeah, I could work with either one of them.

Ms. Lockhart starts reading the pairs of names, "Allen Walker and Christine Brady."

I listen, but my mind wanders all over the place — What's for lunch today? Smells like dog food. How many hours will Mr. Neal let me work this week? You know, I think I can run the whole print shop if he would just —

"Mason Alexander and Rhonda Franks."

My heart's going to jump out of my chest. No way. My ears have to be playing tricks on me. I rewind Ms. Lockhart's voice. Me with Rhonda? That won't work. What am I going to say? What am I going to do? Oh God.

I summon every ounce of strength I have to remain cool. Once the rest of the pairs are called with their assignments, Rhonda slowly turns and smiles at me. It's all I can do to contain myself.

Beads of sweat form and roll down my back. I can feel the looks of envy and cold stares from the few black male faces. Some of the faces are contorted with bewilderment. I also see quick nods of congratulations.

I'm in a position that many of them covet, and they want to see what I'm going to do.

After class, I try to swallow very hard my fear and will my lead-filled legs to walk toward Rhonda. Her back is turned as she scans a book. Once I reach her, I manage to sputter, "Hi."

"Hello."

I run a quick but late mental body check — Is my breath still okay? Are my pits funky? Is there anything in my teeth? Please, no eye or nose boogers. Well, if that's the case, it's too late now.

"It looks like we're going to be working together, huh?" she says.

"Ye-e-s."

"Since we both like this subject, I don't think it will really be "work." She makes quotation marks in the air.

"When do you want to get together?" she asks.

"Anytime."

"What's good for you, Mason?

I'm looking at her, but my mouth isn't moving.

"How about Thursday?"

I nod my head, not really hearing her, but watching her lips move gracefully.

"Great. Let's meet at first lunch."

"Okay," I finally say, hoping I haven't made myself look like an idiot.

"By the way, let me give you my phone number, and I should get yours." She says pulls a pen from the sleeve of her notebook.

Whoa. Nice pen. That's a Sheaffer 727 Imperial. She's got good taste.

"Here you go," she says as she hands me a torn piece of notebook paper with her coveted number.

My knees wobble. I catch them just in time. My heart's pounding. Water's forming on my forehead. My mouth's dry as the Sahara. I clumsily rip a sheet of paper from my notebook, scribble my number and hand it to her.

"Thanks. See you tomorrow in class."

It's a pleasure to watch her walk away.

Wow. I replay the last three minutes of my life over and over. I can't believe this is happening.

Of course now that I've been seen conversing with Rhonda publicly, there'll be an investigation that typically starts with a probing insensitive interrogation. The initial detectives and nosey reporters are naturally the envious guys in the class.

In predictable fashion, right after Rhonda leaves, they surround me. One of them asks bluntly what the rest of them are thinking.

"So what you goin' do man? You gonna hit it or what? She gave you her number. That means she's ready."

My face displays a look of disgust, but I reply with silence and walk away.

I hear one of them say in the distance as I make my way down the hall, "Yep, I told you he was a punk. He's scared of it."

It doesn't take word long to get to my neighborhood crew. On the bus ride home, they conduct their own inquisition. Of course there's Link, who can truly imagine how I feel. Without looking at me, I can sense that he knows how excited I am.

I'm surprised. The grilling from my boys is shorter than I expect. They aren't nearly as crude and rude as the clowns in my class. They don't know how I feel, but strangely, they seem to show respect. They think my pairing with Rhonda is pretty cool and really don't push the matter much. I can't believe they don't resurrect Mitchell's fabulous tale from our summer meeting on the porch. I guess we all knew it was one of his classic fables.

The bus drops us off at our stop. We slap hands, exchange our colloquial pleasantries and head towards our homes.

I sense that Link's lagging behind.

He catches up with me as we cross the street and picks up the conversation about my partnering with Rhonda.

"So what you thinking?" he says.

"Not much."

"C'mon man. I know you. You had a thing for this girl for as long as I can remember, and now you gonna be working with her — for the whole year? You gotta be thinkin' something."

After some rationalizing, I say, "Well, she's fine, nice, and all that, but I don't think she likes me more than a partner and a friend. Besides, she's outta my league. She's one for the pretty boys, you know, the upper crust. Besides, I don't want to get my face cracked. If I say or do anything stupid, it's gonna be a long year."

"Man, I don't' know about that. You gotta have some confidence. She's a girl. You just gotta talk to her. Like my corny ass Uncle Roland says, 'Just be yourself boy.'"

"Right. Get outta here with that mess."

"I've heard some girls talk about you, Mason. You got more goin' for you than you think."

"We'll see what happens." I want to believe his insightful words.

"Confidence bruh. Relax."

"Okay. If you say so."

"I say so. Hey, I meant to ask you. You still reading those mystery books, man? You crack me up. Always trying to figure out the ending — trying to get to the "whodunit" before everybody else. Man, you got me started watchin' them crazy mystery and cop shows — Kojack, Mannix, Perry Mason — and that show's in black and white."

That's me. Cop shows and mysteries. Trying to figure out "the whodunit." The guys hate me for that sometimes. When we watch movies or television shows together that have, as we call it, "a whodunit," I usually figure out who, how, where, and why before they do.

I see Link's eyes widen, and I hear footsteps behind me.

"Hey, Mr. Alexander," Link says.

I turn around.

"Hey, Dad."

"Hey boys. How y'all doin'? How was that first day of school?"

"It was all right. You know, nothin' much happens the first day," Links answers.

"Yeah, it was okay," I add.

My father looks us up and down. Link and I look at each other wondering what in the world he's doing. My father throws his folded newspaper under his arm, puts his curled forefinger to his chin and steps back, studying us a little more.

"Y'all boys look like — seniors," he says, grinning slyly.

Link and I look at each other and watch the grins appear on our faces from my father's affirmation.

"Y'all boys are endin' one phase of yo' lives and about to start another. It's a good time. You got so much to look forward to, and I know y'all are gon' do good — ain't you?"

"Yes, sir," we say.

"What? I can't hear you. I know you can do better than that. Y'all are gon' do good ain't you?"

"Yes, sir!"

"There you go." While pinning the newspaper under his arm, he holds up his dirty, cracked hands in front of us and then points at his tattered boots. "I don't want you boys to ever have to work as hard as I do. You understand me?"

"Yes, sir. We understand."

"Good. Well I'm hungry. Mason, don't you stay out here too long. Link, you probably need to be getting home soon too. Tell Mrs. Potts I said 'Hey.' "

"Yes, sir."

As my father heads to the porch, my sisters burst through the front door and greet him with hugs around his knees and waist.

"Sorry about that, man," I say.

"Sorry about what?"

"My dad and all that corny stuff — us lookin' like seniors, talkin' about his work, you know — "

"Hey. You need to stop with that. Your father's cool."

"Cool? You think so? I don't see it. Cool?"

"Man, you don't know how good you got it. I love my grandmother, but man, what I wouldn't give to have a dad like yours around."

"Really?"

"Hell yeah. I mean — somebody to talk to. Somebody that understands the crazy physical stuff we deal with — you know, 'man stuff.' Somebody to kick yo' ass when you slacking. Somebody who loves you and wants to be with you. You got it good man. Don't take that shit for granted. I'd give anything to have my father around right now. Yours is right here. You can touch him when you want. I think somebody killed mine. Realize what you got man."

Wow. He's right. I do take it for granted my father's always going to be there when I get home. Link has nothing like that. I keep forgetting.

"You're right man. My fault."

"It's cool. You don't have to explain nothing. Man, go read one of yo' 'whodunit' books and relax. Catch you tomorrow. Got Spanish and math homework and it's just the first day. Damn."

"Later."

Evening arrives, and I welcome it with open arms. I lay on my bed mindlessly outlining the ceiling tiles. Link's words pop in my head — "Be yourself. Have confidence." They make so much sense, but I don't see how they can apply to me.

I pull out my calligraphy set and practice a while.

Hey, I'm getting pretty good at Blackletter and Unical. Maybe I can make a little money at lettering.

In a few months, I'll be printing the family holiday cards, so it's never too soon to practice. My hand gets tired.

I crack open another mystery novel, but I don't know how much it's making me relax. Shoot. This is too easy. The ex-husband did it.

***

A few weeks pass and we've been working diligently on our class projects. We're reading black writers — Dubois, Washington, and Douglas. Topics like this are unheard of at a predominantly white southern school like Grimmel, but Rhonda and I have an interest in the area and a good teacher in Ms. Lockhart. Besides, we aren't getting it any place else.

We have to put in some time outside of class. Our school and public library are slim and scarce on the type of resources we need, so we make a few trips to some of the nearby colleges and universities. Some of the teachers also lend us their books.

Rhonda and I are spending a lot of time together, but our conversations are mostly about our project. We chat a about current events, local goings-on in the community and school, but for the most part it's school business.

I still can't help noticing how beautiful she is — inside and out. Even though our relationship is about academics for the most part, I'm still intrigued by her.

The guys in the class continue to dig for nuggets they can exploit. They get nothing. Occasionally my boys ask what's happening with us. I keep telling them that it's all about the schoolwork.

***

It's now October. Things with Rhonda are going well, but I can tell that something's different. She didn't say a lot in the first place, but now she's saying even less. She's not cold or anything like that. Just distant. Aloof. Her body language reflects that something's awry.

Rhonda doesn't hold her head up like she did before. Her posture is guarded and tight. Arms folded defensibly. Fallen countenance. The twinkle in those dark brown eyes and brightness in her smile have diminished.

Today is so blah and stagnant. Everything and everybody is just going through the motions, hoping to make it to the end of the day and start over tomorrow.

We've been working hard most of the day but hit a wall and decide to call it quits. As we leave the classroom, I summon the courage to ask, "Is everything okay?"

Without looking up from the book she's scanning, she responds, "Yes," and quickly directs the conversation back to the project.

"I'm sorry for being so nosey."

"No apology necessary. Thanks for asking. Everything's 'okay.' " She makes her quotation marks in the air. I've learned air quotation marks are typical Rhonda, but I sense that everything is not okay.

Although for the past couple of months we've been working and conversing about our schoolwork, I know enough about Rhonda that she's not being honest and something's definitely off. I honor her response to my question, and leave it alone — for the moment.

Her actions change even more over the next couple of weeks, which make me pay closer attention. My feelings for her are running deeper than teenage infatuation. But if nothing ever happens between us, we're at least becoming friends. That's closer than I've ever been to her. I can live with that, and right now I know my friend is dealing with something.

***

A crisp afternoon finds us walking to Rhonda's house from the library. I can see that today is really tough for her. She speaks in monosyllables. She isn't present at all. But what catches my attention are her trembling hands and fingers struggling to hold the books in her tightly folded arms.

She stares ahead blankly, and a tear trickles from her right eye and splashes on her wrist.

I stop.

"Rhonda, are you all right?" I ask, not sure what to do or expect.

She stops too and looks at me. Her face is filled with deep despair, fear, and agony. Her eyes well and overflow like broken levees. Her voice cracks, unsuccessfully attempting to choke back sobs.

"No, I'm not. I-I can't take it anymore."

I take the books from her arms and combine them with mine and guide her by her arm to a soft spot of grass on an incline by the curb.

We sit.

"What do you mean you can't take it anymore? What's going on? Take what anymore?"

By now she's sobbing heavily. I'm concerned, confused, and at a loss for what to do.

Between deep breaths and sobs she manages to say, "I can't tell you."

I assure her that she can trust me and I can handle anything, even though I have no idea whether I can or not.

I'm really nervous, and my mind tries to quickly analyze and deduce what the problem might be. Was she sick? Had someone hurt her? I don't see any visible signs on her face or the rest of her exposed extremities. Did she do something wrong? Please, not Rhonda.

My mind exhausts all the ideas and possibilities it can muster. Nothing makes sense.

I decide to follow some advice my grandmother gave me regarding people who are upset.

Sometimes you don't say anything. You're just there for them. Shut up and be there.

I stop talking.

I put our books down on the grass, slide next to Rhonda, gently put my arm around her and we rock slowly — saying absolutely nothing. The world stops to rock with us.

A gentle breeze makes crimson and orange leaves dance to give her comfort, and to say that no matter what, everything will be okay. With the exception of the foliage ballet, there's silence.

I don't know what's wrong, but as I hold her she trembles. I can sense that she's hurting, confused, and scared.

As we continue to rock, I feel some of the tension in her body release. Her crying stops.

"Thank you," she whispers and wipes her eyes.

In the midst of my armchair psychoanalysis and our rocking, I forgot that I have a handkerchief. Thank goodness it's clean.

She dries her tears and thanks me.

"You're such a good friend, Mason," she says, her nose red, eyes puffy and glassy.

Here we go — another punch in the face. But I realize that the f-word doesn't sound so bad coming from her. It feels more like a platform to launch upward from instead of a ceiling.

I don't probe anymore. We gather our things and finish the walk to her house. I stand on the sidewalk and give a quick wave goodbye as she closes the front door.

An eerie feeling comes over me. Somewhere in that old white A-framed home with the black shutters lay the root of what caused Rhonda's meltdown today. I don't know what it is, but certainly it's in there.

CHAPTER FOUR

It's one of those rare warm October Saturday afternoons — an Indian summer day. And we decide to spend it at Craven Park. I stand on the edge of the basketball court waiting for the game to end. It's 20-20. Next point wins. Marshall, Dep, and I are up next. Link doesn't feel like running with us. He's at the other end of the park getting to know, as he put it, "a pretty little redbone" he just met. I get lost in watching the guys running and sweating profusely to score the last shot and be a hero. Some try to show off their skills for the girls. Others need to find something else to do besides play ball.

The warm weather brought a lot of folks to Craven today. People sit on their cars, doors open, windows down, conversing and watching the games. Car stereos blast R&B from WGML. Lots of libations are being consumed. Reefer burning in the far corner of the parking lot wafts my way.

To be a teenager in Grimmel.

Then it hits me. I won't be in this spot next year or maybe ever again. I won't be anywhere around here. My pending departure becomes sobering, exciting, and scary. But I'm starting to feel ready.

I reminisce about how I reached his point.

The first thing that comes to mind is college applications. Boy, I hate those things. Who can really know anything about a person from a biographical sketch that anybody could have written, scores from biased standardized tests — and you're screwed if you're having a bad day on the day of the exam — high school transcripts filled with inflated grades, and flowery, over exaggerated letters of recommendation?

I have no choice but to play the game if I want to go to college.

We have school guidance counselors to "help," but ours really don't listen. Maybe they can't hear. Whatever the problem is, they think they know everything, talk constantly, and say absolutely nothing.

To make matters worse, our counselors are old and white. I don't have anything against them being white, but that combined with their funky condescending attitude doesn't help at all. When we talk, if you want to call it that, it's like we're speaking different languages.

I told Mrs. Gallagher I liked architecture and commercial design and wanted to study one of them in college. This ancient wrinkled walking skeleton disagreed and decided to "guide" me in another direction.

"You have discipline, young man. Forget about college and go in the Army."

I screamed like Bruce Lee, leaped over the desk and kicked Mrs. Gallagher in the throat. The force knocked her out of her chair into the bookcase. Books, coffee, files, and papers went flying. I walked over to her desk, and there she was, on the floor, head over heels, her dress over her face, showing more than anyone ever wanted to see.

Well that's what I imagined doing.

Mrs. Gallagher just sat there peering at me with this stupid look on her face, like she delivered some great prophecy regarding my life.

This woman wasted 15 minutes of both our lives, and from the looks of her, she didn't have 15 minutes to spare.

How in the world could she go from me saying I wanted to study architecture or commercial design to sending me to the Army? I never let the word form on my lips. What an insult.

I hear Marshall say, "Mason, let's go. We're up." The game is finally over. Time to go play some ball.

Thankfully, all of us who're planning to go to college have allies in Reverend and Mrs. Tremmel.

Ah, the Tremmels. They're incredible. Both went to college and know how to navigate the game. It's important to them that anyone who wants to go to college gets all the help and tools they need. The Tremmels have made the third Wednesday of each month school night at Mt. Sinai. Some of the teachers in the congregation, along with Rev. and Mrs. Tremmel, help with homework and preparing college applications.

Reverend Tremmel was beside himself when he learned I was applying to Maryland State University. It's his alma mater, and he has no problem sharing how proud he is of MSU — "his place of matriculation." My application submission adds another feather to his cap and expands his chest and head a little more.

Rev. Tremmel can go on and on about his college days, fraternity life, favorite teachers, the plethora of beautiful women, and countless epic tales about nearly any subject with college you can imagine. Although he's told some of his stories more than once with a bit more seasoning depending on his mood, we still enjoy hearing and watching him tell them.

I'm a good student so Rev. Tremmel wrote glowing letters of recommendation for me and even put in a good word with some of the people that he knew who were still at Maryland State. I know that he's softly urging me in the direction of going there. I don't want him to know, but it's my top choice.

Ironically, Mrs. Sonya Tremmel, or as we nicknamed her, Ms. Sonya — we knew she was married, but that moniker flowed off our tongues — went to her husband's rival, Maryland University-Baltimore. The two met early in their college years, but were able to get along despite the rivalry. She too is very happy I'm considering Maryland State and wishes me all the best — even if it's the enemy school.

For the most part, all of the neighborhood crew go to churches in the area, but we all have connections with Mt. Sinai — Vacation Bible School, lock-ins, summer BBQs, Easter egg hunts, countless plays, and Sunday School. Even though we're older now, we still manage to make it to some of those events.

Mt. Sinai is a staple of the community. All are welcomed — members or not — especially children and young adults. It's a great place to be and we take full advantage.

I remember when Reverend Dexter and Sonya Lynne Tremmel came to our town. They made a striking impression on everyone as soon as they crossed the threshold of our little sanctuary.

Rev. Tremmel's a remarkably handsome man. His skin is light and has a reddish bronze tint. His facial features are a proportionate mix of African, Native American, and Caucasian, which gives him a distinctive mysterious look. His bluish-green eyes seem to hold a sense of wisdom, a kind of hypnotic power, and at the same time, a street slickness. His hair is dark brown and wavy — the color matches his pencil moustache.

I was a little boy when they came, maybe five or six so his six-feet-four-inch frame made him look like a big red giant to me.

Bachelors and seminary degrees gave him immediate credibility with the educators in the church and local community, and since he's a fraternity man, he connected with the college-educated women, men and masons. He oozes charisma and charm.

Rev. Tremmel was in his early to mid-30s when he became Mt. Sinai's pastor about 11 years ago, but he's not your typical black Baptist preacher.

We were used to seeing the fried chicken eating, big stomach having, erroneous Bible quoting caricatures. Rev. Tremmel is the antithesis of this.

He's fit, in good shape, and doesn't speak like a wannabe Martin Luther King, Jr. He knows when to use slang, and can speak the King's English better than Ms. Lockhart. He runs with the kids in impromptu races after church — and sometimes wins. When he has time, he plays softball with Mt. Sinai's team in the Yellowstone County church league, shoots basketball with the older teenagers and adults, and is the constant recipient of double-takes and harmless, but flirtatious hugs and pats from a good number of the women in the church.

The majority of the congregation loved Rev. Tremmel from the beginning.

It's funny. Even when I was a little fellow and didn't understand everything that was happening, I can remember vividly Deacon Cleotis Johnson jumping up in the church meeting to hire Rev. Tremmel and yelling, "Don't do it. I don't like him." I thought the members were going to kill him.

He got into it with Mr. Walker.

"Johnson, leave that man alone. Rev. Tremmel ain't done nothing to you," Mr. Walker said. "You don't even know him, and you swear he's up to no good."

"I know he ain't done nothing to me, but I know he ain't up to no good. I told y'all before he first got here that he was slick, but you said I was crazy. I saw it when he came to visit. I'm tellin' y'all, he don't treat that wife a his right."

"How do you know?"

"I can just tell. I got eyes. I can see things."

"Shut up, Johnson." Mr. Walker yelled.

Mr. Johnson didn't shut up.

"How y'all gon' bring in somebody to lead you, and you don't check 'em out first? I'm not the only one that says you need to check him out. Y'all said Mrs. Potts was crazy too. Y'all gon' see soon enough. He ain't what y'all think he is."

Mr. Walker motioned to two large men sitting in the back of the church. They moved quickly and flanked Johnson. Without touching him, they escorted Mr. Johnson out of the meeting. As he made his way to the door he yelled, "Y'all better leave that fool alone. He ain't right. He ain't right. Tell 'em Potts. Tell 'em.

I saw some folks looking at the floor and nodding lightly in agreement with Mr. Johnson's proclamations — in particular, Mrs. Potts, Link's grandmother, who he called out to. But none of them said anything out loud. It didn't matter. It was a nearly unanimous vote to hire Rev. Tremmel.

Mr. Johnson doesn't have too many fans at Mt. Sinai. Most folks have tagged him as the number one hater of Rev. Tremmel. It's as if he goes out of his way to oppose almost everything Rev. Tremmel proposes. He's usually alone on an island.

Rev. Tremmel has that special something. That "it" factor — that thing that pulls people to him like a magnet. His firm handshakes and tight hugs combined with the intoxicating mix of Old Spice and Brute colognes make you feel special. When he talks to you, he has this knack of making you feel as if there's no other person in the world more important than you.

The man had everyone under his spell the first time he said, "Tremmel rhymes with Grimmel, and this is where I'm supposed to be." They still eat that up.

His voice commands respect from the congregation. There's no Tremmel sermon that isn't engaging and funny.

The big plus for many of the older members is the fact that Rev. Tremmel is married. A few men worried that their wives and other female church members would pay unnecessary attention to a single pastor and had concerns about him being overwhelmed by female callers.

Knowing that there was a Mrs. Tremmel dismissed those worries.

Most of the guys in our group think a lot of Rev. Tremmel. His actions when BJ terrorized us showed us that he was true to his word and wasn't just giving lip service. In some ways we even try to emulate his cool strut and the way he talks.

Ms. Sonya is absolutely beautiful. Her skin is mocha, smooth and unblemished. Thick, black, straight, soft hair, when not in a bun, grazes the bottoms of her shoulder blades.

Her eyes are large, round and captivating like deep brown pools. Full lips and a beautifully shaped broad nose fit her face perfectly, accentuating her high cheekbones. Ms. Sonya's about 5' 5" and has a shape that women envy and makes men study longer than they should. She doesn't wear a lot of form-fitting clothes, but anyone can see her bodacious curves, firm round backside, and full bosom.

She too, is probably in her early to mid-thirties.

"Reverend and Mrs. Tremmel just dropped out of heaven." I heard my mother say. "God truly sent them to us."

I don't know what to think about all of that. I just know that speaking for us young people, we love them, and they make church fun.

Ms. Sonya teaches the young kids Sunday school class. She creates games that help us get the gist of popular Bible stories, and we develop our reading and public speaking skills.

There's always some program or place in church services that requires one of us younger folks to say a memorized poem, read from the Bible, or give a speech. I don't really like doing this stuff, but I understand why she does it. Only for Ms. Sonya.

In my pre-teen years, I used Ms. Sonya's Sunday school reading class time to exercise some of my personal vendettas.

There were guys my age and a little older who liked to bully and threaten some of us smaller kids. These were the guys that would put you in a headlock or full nelson in front of everybody and make you say or do something silly before they'd let you go. Something like — "Say 'I like to wear my mama's drawers.' Say it or I'll kick yo' butt."

They might trip you, grab your wrists and make you hit yourself with your hands. They might push you and make you fall down, or say derogatory things loudly about you, your clothes, or your physical features. I hated it most when they put you in a nonexistent relationship with somebody undesirable, all just to make you look bad. "Hey y'all, Mason go with Toni. I saw them kissin' behind the shed." Toni was the girl that always smelled like pee. I liked Toni, but when you're a little boy, you don't want to be put with the pee girl.

Most of the bullies were overgrown behemoths, so fighting wasn't the first option to get back at them. But I found that Ms. Sonya's class provided opportunities to enact my revenge.

At some point she made us all read from the Bible or the lesson book. Most of them couldn't read or spell well at all, so when Ms. Sonya called on them, I'd giggle my ass off.

I'd giggle just loud enough for them to hear me. It was so much fun hearing them spit, sputter, and stammer their way through sentences trying to say words like "p-p-piece," "s-s-s-savior," and "m-m-m-messiah." I'd almost choke if they encountered any word with more than three syllables.

If Ms. Sonya asked us to help them, I gladly, loudly, and sarcastically blurted out the correct answer. Hearing these wannabe tough guys stutter and stumble was better than hitting them with my fists. I understand that it's not right, but it was such guilty pleasure and bloodless revenge.

I'm sure Ms. Sonya knew about my surreptitious vengeance, but she never let anyone know. I can't prove it, but I swear that she smiled at me once when she heard me do this. That was the day my crush on Ms. Sonya started.

The Tremmels brought our little country church into the 20th century. People come from miles away to hear what Rev. Tremmel has to say and to witness the changes.

I couldn't understand everything he preached about when I was younger, but I'm getting better. He doesn't beat us to death about Jesus. He talks about being black and proud. He tells us about Africa, Africans, slavery, knowing our history, respect for all people, and how to treat each other.

Conversations in the congregation about his approach were mixed at first. Some loved his radical non-traditional ideas. It challenged people to think about the community, who they are, and their history.

Others thought he was too full of himself. To them he was another slick jackleg preacher who talks too much about that black stuff.

"He needs to preach Jesus and leave that other mess alone," some said.

Rev. Tremmel keeps working no matter what and people keep coming. He's even bringing naysayers around — a little.

Mt. Sinai isn't large — physically or in membership — by any means. The average attendance before the Tremmels was 15-20 people on a good Sunday, not including the four or five people in the choir. Now each Sunday we're squeezed to capacity — 250 — often with standing room only.

Ms. Sonya does her part as well. She organizes the youth, Sunday school, tutoring, and works to unite Mt. Sinai and the community. Some of her efforts are also met with scathing critiques too, but her work is fruitful.

Ms. Sonya and Rev. Tremmel make a wonderful team. It's something to see and be a part of. So much is happening.

Not only do the Tremmels work hard and push us, but they also make sure that we have opportunities to make good times and precious memories.

***

The summer church trips with the Tremmels are the best. This summer was no different. It was special because I got to know Ms. Sonya in a different way.

The trips have been going on since I can remember, and the Tremmels, mostly Ms. Sonya, have made sure they've been good ones. She organizes these short pleasure journeys for the youth, but lots of adults go as well. They take us to zoos, plays, and concerts. But this year we went to our favorite spot — Livingstone Amusement Park, or as we call it — the LAP.

We took the three-hour trek to Coswell, Georgia on a *Greenways* 46-seater–with a bathroom. Fancy stuff.

It's always hot and muggy when we go to the LAP, and this summer continues the tradition. It doesn't matter though. We're let loose for six hours, with a few dollars and pinned up energy in what we interpret as a wonderland.

After all the years of church trips and bus rides, that morning I found myself sitting next to Ms. Sonya for two hours.

This lady is phenomenal. She's so easy on the eyes. I hope she didn't catch me staring. Man, if she and Rev. Tremmel weren't married and I was a little older, I'd have to stand in a long line. But it would be worth the wait. She smells good too. That morning she smelled like cocoa butter and apple blossoms.

The bus lurched forward from the gears changing as it exited the church parking lot. Out of the corner of my eye I saw Ms. Sonya's breasts jiggle. Wow. The sliver of visible cleavage hypnotized me momentarily.

Mason. Mason. Get it together. That's not you. You're a good guy. You don't do that — but damn she's fine.

At the time Ms. Sonya was looking ahead to see what was going on with the driver. That gave me a second to adjust my sight to where it was supposed to be.

When the bus reached the highway, she and I chatted about some of everything — sports — yes, Ms. Sonya likes sports. She loves basketball. She also likes music. Parliament-Funkadelic? James Brown? Ms. Sonya's hipper than I thought. She told me about the Parliament-Funkadelic show that she and Rev. Tremmel went to a little while ago.

"George Clinton is crazy." she said, throwing her head back and laughing as she re-lived the memory.

"The man never gets tired. You should've seen the Mothership come down from the top of the coliseum. It was so wild. The guitar player had on a diaper. The horns were blowing. The drummer had these sticks that glow in the dark. They were so funky."

She made me feel like I was there.

Ha. Ms. Sonya said "funky." She's so cool.

The conversation shifted.

"So Mr. Alexander, what's this with you and Ms. Franks?" she asked.

That was a surprise. I didn't think she knew or noticed anything about that.

I tried to keep from smiling but I couldn't.

"Ms. Sonya, shh." I pressed my fingers to my lips to emphasize my request.

"She's in the back."

I looked hard out of the corner of my eye and tilted my head a little so I could see the back of the bus. Rhonda didn't hear anything. Thankfully, she and Cheryl Brown were deep in conversation. Rhonda's was making air quotations, so the subject must be enjoyable.

Rhonda's not an official member of our church. But she and some of my other friends often go with us to different outings.

Eventually, I responded to her question: "Nothing much. We're partners in Ms. Lockhart's English class. You know — not much."

"Hmm. Not much? Okay. So how's the work going?"

"Good — I guess."

"You guess? You don't know?"

"Well I–"

"Come now, Mason."

"Okay. The work's going good, but — "

"But what?"

I looked at the roof. I stole a quick glance at Rhonda. She and Cheryl were still talking. I knew what Ms. Sonya was getting at, and she was breaking me down.

"I like her." There. I said it. I confessed. "Ms. Sonya," I begged, "please don't say anything."

"Don't worry Mason. I'd never do that. So have you told — "

"No ma'am."

"And why not?"

Is she crazy.

"No way. I'll just keep that to myself."

"Think about telling her. She might surprise you."

"And if she embarrasses me?"

"She won't. I'm a woman. I can tell."

"You definitely are a woman, but I've heard that before," I mumbled to myself.

"But if she doesn't like you like that, it's okay.

"You're a good young man. Everything will work out just fine.

Link said the same thing.

"So, you're going to ride The Raging Beast with me, right?"

"Okay Ms. Sonya. But only for you."

***

We pulled into the crowded LAP parking lot. It was barely 10 a.m. but buses, cars, and a sea of people gathered to besiege the park. The peaks of The Raging Beast, one of the most feared roller coasters in the South, peaked over the walls, beckoning us.

Rev. Tremmel stood in the front of the bus and yelled directions about what time we're supposed to eat and be back to return to Grimmel. After his command to "Have fun," people shot off the bus past him, destined to conquer the park.

I lagged behind, waiting for Ms. Sonya.

Rhonda and Cheryl waved as they passed me on their way to the entrance.

Rhonda. Pink shorts. White halter top. Ponytail tied with a pink band. Tanned legs.

Oh my goodness.

Ms. Sonya stepped off the bus. White shorts. Tight peach short-sleeved blouse tied at the waist. Leather sandals with beige straps wrapped around her ankles and calves. Dark shades. Summer tan.

Wow. If Rev. Tremmel only knew what some of the guys were thinking.

Then it clicked. I realized at that moment how alike Ms. Sonya and Rhonda are. The way they walk. They're both slightly bowlegged and their feet turn in a little when they stand. Their kindness and thoughtfulness is immeasurable. What man wouldn't want a woman like that?

I honored my promise that day to Ms. Sonya and rode The Raging Beast with her. There were a lot of people, but the line moved fast. I didn't let her know, but I was more afraid than she was. We sat in the third car of six. As the train of cars shook and chugged slowly up the steep incline, chains clanging, everything below getting smaller and smaller, Ms. Sonya turned to me and asked, "Are you ready?"

"Yes." I replied, lying through my teeth.

If there had been an exit button, I would have beaten it to death.

The front car finally reached the top of the hill. There was a dramatic pause. It felt like the world stood still, and then — *whoosh*. We went straight down. I saw tracks coming up fast to meet me. The big drop sent my stomach to my mouth. She screamed at the top of her lungs, and I clutched the rail for dear life. Curves, flips, dips, moments of nearly losing my breakfast and bowels. I didn't breathe until the cars stopped at the end of the ride.

Wow. I'm still alive.

"Thank you, Mason. You're such a gentleman."

I wanted to kiss the ground.

"You're welcome. It was a lot of fun." I lied again.

"Now get out of here and find your friends." She gave my cheek a kiss. That sent me on my way.

I definitely wouldn't do that for anybody but Ms. Sonya.

In my search to find Dep and Marshall, the rest of the guys didn't make the trip — I saw Rhonda and Cheryl again.

My mind quickly flashed to a couple of years ago when Mr. Johnson caught Cheryl in the woods by the LAP — bus parking area with some boy from Roseboro County Baptist.

People in the congregation are right. Mr. Johnson is as ornery as they come. It's as if he's constantly expecting somebody, especially teenagers, to do something that he thinks isn't right. He's at every church function and I don't think he's missed any of our trips to the LAP — at least that I can remember. But the man is like a ninja. He pops out of nowhere trying to catch and chastise people doing something he thinks they shouldn't.

Mr. Johnson pegged Cheryl just before we were about to leave the LAP. He pulled her by the arm back to the bus and told Rev. Tremmel in front of everybody, "This fast child was over there bein' nasty. She and that boy was over there in them woods fumbling with each other."

He couldn't have embarrassed Cheryl any more.

"I'll deal with it, Johnson," Rev. Tremmel said.

"Well see that you do. And you need to tend to yo' own business too."

Everyone gathered around, listening, expecting a retort from Rev. Tremmel. Instead, he just looked at Johnson sideways, smiled, and walked Cheryl to the bus.

Mr. Walker approached Mr. Johnson from behind and said, "You always trying to start something with Rev. Tremmel. You need to stop it."

"Aww, y'all need to stop it. Y'all know how fast that girl is."

"I'm not talking about Cheryl. I'm talking about what you said to Rev. Tremmel."

Mr. Johnson swatted at the air, as if he were wiping away Mr. Walker's words.

"I don't care what y'all say, that man ain't right. Keep on bein' stupid. I done told y'all."

The crowd dispersed during Mr. Johnson's diatribe and made their way to the bus.

I could see Rev. Tremmel talking to Cheryl by the side of the bus. She nodded in response to his words. He gave her a hug, and she boarded the bus.

Even though folks didn't like what Mr. Johnson did, Cheryl had to take that long walk down the bus aisle past everyone back to her seat. No one said anything out loud, but you could feel the depth of accusations and wonderings.

It took a long time for the jokes about Cheryl to stop. They did eventually, but she'll never live it down completely, thanks to Mr. Johnson.

This time there were no "being nasty" incidents. We had a ball eating and riding everything. I even stood in line with Cheryl and Rhonda for their fourth ride on the rollercoaster. I sat next to Ms. Sonya for the trip home, but we didn't talk as much. Sleep rolled our heads like marbles and made our mouths hang open. The park beat us up pretty good, but I loved every minute.

Parents that didn't make the trip were waiting for us as we pulled into the parking lot that evening. As Ms. Sonya gathered her things, she reminded me of our conversation about Rhonda. I smiled and exited the bus.

I saw Rhonda wave to everyone as she closed the door of Ms. Franks' '73 Plymouth Fury.

Another great time and set of memories courtesy of the Tremmels. There won't be many more like this, so I cherish every moment. I know it's all going to change soon enough.

CHAPTER FIVE

"Hello? Good afternoon to you to Rev. Tremmel. We're doin' just fine," I hear my mother say. "Yes he is. Hold on a minute. Mason. Telephone. It's Rev. Tremmel."

Rev. Tremmel? Calling me? It's not the first time, but what in the world could he want? Last Sunday was Youth Sunday.

The curled baby blue phone cord stretches from the kitchen. My mother hands me the receiver, as I enter the hallway.

Whack.

My baby sister punches me in the thigh and runs down the hall laughing.

"Hello?"

"Hey, Mason. How's everything?"

"Pretty good."

"Hey, look, the reason I'm calling is I want to use your artistic expertise — specifically your calligraphy skills. I need to make some posters for a conference and write some important letters, and I want to use a nice lettering style. You're the only other person I know that can write as well as me."

Really? Rev. Tremmel's okay at calligraphy, but he's not as good as he thinks he is.

"I don't have time to do them all, so can you — "

"Yes, sir. I've been practicing Blackletter and Unical. When do you want me to do this?"

"Blackletter and Unical — yeah," he says.

He has no idea what I'm talking about.

"Okay. How's later today? I know it's Saturday, but if you're free, we could do it today."

"Uh, hmm. I can meet you at 1 at the church. Is that okay?" I ask.

"Sure. I'll see you in about a half an hour. Thanks Mason. I appreciate it."

I hang up the phone and head to my room. I hear my father climb out of his recliner.

"What you fixin' to do Mason?" my father asks.

"Rev. Tremmel asked me to do some calligraphy for him, and I'm going to meet — ".

"Okay, but let me tell you something. I like Tremmel and everything, but don't let that man or nobody else use you. You need to make sure he pays you."

I hadn't thought about that.

"You always want to get paid for your time and talent. You doin' personal stuff for him. It's okay to get paid. You need to get paid."

"Okay. Thanks, Dad."

My baby sister is in the kitchen engrossed in combing her doll's hair and doesn't see me come behind her. I flip her upside down and give her stomach a raspberry and tickle under her arms. She squeals with delight. I put her gently on the floor.

"That's what you get for punching my leg."

She's still laughing as I grab my calligraphy set off the kitchen table and head out the back door.

It's a short jog to the church.

***

Rev. Tremmel's in his office.

"Right on time." he says when I walk in. "I like that."

We lay out the materials. Looks like we're ready to go.

Uh oh. He's opening drawers and rifling through his briefcase with a concerned look on his face.

"Darn it. I'm out of indigo blue ink. Do you have any, Mason?"

"No sir. I only have black."

"I got to have indigo blue. Darn it. Well it looks like we need to make a run to the art store. You got time?"

"Yes, sir."

"Let's go."

We hop in his '78 black Monte Carlo parked just outside his study.

The art store is in the Maple Leaf Mall in Rellingsway, which is about 25 minutes away.

It's a beautiful day, and I'm hanging out with Rev. Tremmel.

"So how's school, Mace?" he asks. I'm not a big fan of him calling me Mace. Thankfully, he only does it every now and then. Hey, it's Rev. Tremmel, so I let it slide.

"Pretty good. We're reading a lot of authors you and Ms. Sonya told us about."

"Oh yeah? That's great."

"Yes, sir. I was surprised too."

"Good. Get as much as you can out of the work."

"I will."

"So, what's going on with you and the ladies?"

Uh oh. I don't want to talk about this subject with him. I look out of the passenger window at the trees whizzing by, folks working in their yards, and the open fields.

I finally respond.

"Not much."

"Oh man. This is my cut." he says excitedly, turning up the radio. I don't think he heard my response, or he really didn't care about my answer.

He sings loudly along with the music — it's "Get Off" by Foxy.

He's into it. Head bobbing. He knows every whisper of the song. Rev. Tremmel looks at me and smiles. I feel myself force my lips to respond. I don't know what to feel at this moment. I know the song, and I like it, but I feel strange listening to it with — Rev. Tremmel. And he's singing the lyrics — loudly. This is definitely a side of him I've never seen before.

Can we just get to the store?

Maple Leaf is crowded as usual for a Saturday afternoon, but we find a parking space near the north entrance, a few doors down from the art store.

Walking through the mall with all of these people is a chore, but I'm focused. I'm on a mission. I'm working with Rev. Tremmel on some important stuff.

It's not unusual to see Rev. Tremmel without his collar. But today he's wearing white Converse All-Stars, jeans, a really cool orange and black Maryland State University T-shirt and a black baseball cap. He's still Rev. Tremmel, but this is the ultra cool version. He's a cat I want to be seen with.

As we walk, I notice that Rev. Tremmel's mind isn't focused. Neither is his vision. He's eyeing every girl and woman that walks by. I can't believe it. I know he's a guy just like me. And I can see all the pretty ladies in the mall too. I look at them. But I swear Rev. Tremmel's undressing them with his eyes and more.

Strangely, no one seems to notice what he's doing except me.

I feel a little uneasy watching his head swivel back and forth, up and down. I'm expecting drool to drip from his mouth any second.

What really bothers me is that when one very attractive, well-built young woman just a few years older than me walks by us, he visually rapes her. Then he looks at me for approval, raising his eyebrows up and down and tilting his head in the direction the lady walks.

"What you think about that?" he asks. "Grade A Beef, huh?"

I shrug and look down, "I guess so."

"Right. Boy you know that girl's finer than frog's hair. I bet you have fun with girls like that all the time don't you?"

He's listening now.

"I guess."

"What about Rhonda? Ms. Sonya told me that you're teamed up with her for a school project. So what's happening?"

"What do you mean?"

"C'mon son. Both her and her mother are foxes. Boy, if I was you —"

"No, Rev. Tremmel. It's nothing like that."

My facial expression and eyes don't move. He seems to sense my uneasiness.

"Okay. Okay, Mason."

He gazes in front of him, continuing his search through the mass of people for more "Grade A Beef."

We finally arrive at the art store.

I love looking at pretty girls as much as the next guy, but I think there's a way to do it. The way Rev. Tremmel violated these women is disrespectful not only to them but also to Ms. Sonya. His wife is as pretty if not prettier than everybody we've seen in the mall. Did he forget she's waiting for him at home?

His reckless eyeballing and flippant attitude leave a peculiar mark on the lens through which I see him.

We get back to his office and finish the work. Rev. Tremmel was right. The indigo blue works really well. I can't tell him, but his writing needs some work though. The spacing on "E" and "F" are rough. Nevertheless, between the two of us, we churn out some quality posters and letters. Anyone that can see can tell the differences in the work, and so can Rev. Tremmel if he's honest. Still, his is passable.

I get ready to leave and hear my father's words. I'm certain that Rev. Tremmel is going to offer me something. I probably won't take it, but I'm sure he'll make an offer.

He doesn't.

It bothers me that I gave up my Saturday for him and this man doesn't offer a dime.

My father's words ring loud. It looks like he was right — people will try to use you.

I hem, haw, trying to give him a chance to do the right thing. He doesn't get it. So I create an opening for him.

"Man, those calligraphy supplies aren't cheap are they?" I ask.

"Yeah, they do add up. That ink was more than I expected."

Rev. Tremmel continues organizing the papers on his desk.

"I understand. I just bought some new nibs and paper. It hit my pocket pretty hard."

He finally catches on.

"Oh yeah Mason. I'll straighten you out with a little change — say fifty dollars. Can I get it to you next week. How's that?"

"That sounds good, Rev Tremmel. I appreciate it. Thanks. I'll see you Sunday."

I waste no time getting out of there.

As I jog home, Rev. Tremmel's actions have my emotions all over the place, and now questions about him are assaulting my mind. Is this the same guy who talks to us about treating people with dignity? Why did he ogle those girls like that? And why did he want me to cosign what he did in the mall? Why did he say that about Rhonda and her mother? I don't know what to think.

Is that Mr. Johnson? He's walking towards me as I jog home. It's 7:30. I wonder where he's headed this evening. As I get closer to him, he waves. What's this? It's usually like pulling teeth to get him to speak, especially to speak first. He stops.

"Hey son," he says. He shakes my hand. I'm shocked. Mr. Johnson is cleaned up — shirt, slacks, fresh shave.

Interesting.

"Where you headed in such a hurry?" he asks.

I'm flabbergasted. Mr. Cleotis Johnson is asking me a question about myself and isn't chastising me? Whoa.

"Home. I was working with Rev. Tremmel on a — "

"Rev. Tremmel? Hmmph." he responds. "You doin' all right?"

I'm blown away.

"Yes, sir. Are you feeling well?"

"I sure am," he says as he heads on down the sidewalk. I could swear Mr. Johnson is skipping. I wonder where he's headed. I start jogging again. Oh shit. It hits me. Mrs. Emma Winston lives down that way.

CHAPTER SIX

Mt. Sinai's reputation continues to grow in the community, and the little church is helping to shape us into the women and men we should become.

Some of us are entering the crux of our teen years. Life is changing for us. We've graduated from Ms. Sonya's elementary church school classes.

We still laugh about him catching Cheryl "being nasty" with that boy at the LAP, and she even laughs about it now. That'll never get old. I'm not sure, but I think I've seen Marshall checking out Cheryl. I'll have to ask him about that.

Now I have my own experience with Mr. Johnson. I remember him ratting out Cheryl, but I've seen another Mr. Johnson — one talking to me, one actually having a smile on his face as he skipped to Mrs. Winston's — to get a piece. I can't believe I'd nearly forgotten about that. I can't believe I haven't told the guys. Slick Mr. Johnson.

But as a Sunday school teacher, Mr. Johnson's a pain in the ass. Out of respect for our elders, we never say anything ugly about him within earshot, but we've created a library of what we think are hilarious jokes about his age and his first name.

Dep came up with, "Johnson's so old he gave Adam his first haircut."

Mr. Johnson's probably in his 60s or early 70s — and that's ancient to us.

Link said, "Who in the world would name their child Cleotis? Sounds like some left over slave name his folks used to punish him. Or it's a bad mispronunciation of a female body part."

Maybe he knows his name is messed up and he takes it out on us.

We're not fans of his. For the most part it's because he's so cranky most of the time, but it's mainly because he and Rev. Tremmel don't get along. He's usually on the other side of anything Rev. Tremmel does. But members of the congregation quickly defend him when Mr. Johnson says something derogatory.

I don't think Mr. Johnson likes children very much — especially teenagers. It's that or he does an excellent job of acting like he doesn't.

We can't believe Johnson volunteered to be a teacher in the youth department. His supposed teaching is always a 60-minute tirade about today's young folks.

"Why y'all wear yo' hair so long? Can't tell who's a girl or boy."

At some point, the phrase "Back in my day," introduces one of his dry stories.

"Y'all need to talk like ya got some sense. All these words like, 'funky' and 'Right on.' That's nonsense. You can't get no job talkin' like that. What's the matter which ya? Boy, what kinda shoes you got on? Look like you got on high heels. Just ain't biblical."

How he connects these and other accusations to the Bible still baffles me.

According to Mr. Johnson, the way we act, dress and talk will be the demise and degradation of the black community. Basically, he says we won't amount to much of anything, and we're bound for hell if we don't get it together.

"Better straighten up and fly right." is his favorite saying.

Johnson's a piece of work, but there's some sincerity in what he's trying to convey.

Still, I do my best to never go to his class. If my mother didn't make me, I'd never go.

One Sunday, Marshall was visiting our Sunday school and church service. It was one of those Sundays we're going to have dinner afterwards, and the way this skinny dude can eat is unbelievable. Mt. Sinai is famous for its great cooks and delectable food, and they always prepare more than enough. Marshall wasn't going to miss this opportunity.

It seemed like everyone in Grimmel knew Mr. Johnson didn't like Rev. Tremmel, but most of us young folks just accepted it and went on. Well, I have no idea what or why Marshall did what he did, but while we were in Mr. Johnson's class, out of the blue, Marshall raised his hand to ask a question. Of course, Mr. Johnson was in the midst of one his angry soliloquies but saw Marshall's hand waving in the air.

"Yes, young man? What is it?"

Marshall stared at him blankly and asked, "I was just wondering. Why do you hate Rev. Tremmel?"

The class gasped. We almost died.

We all knew he didn't like him, but would never dare to ask why. He looked at Marshall as though Marshall had kicked him in the face.

Mr. Johnson managed to keep his face blank but his stammering gave him away. "Well-uh-er-son-that's none of — What? You need to stay out of grown folks business."

We were paralyzed. What in the world was happening?

"Okay," Marshall said. "Let me ask you something that is my business. Are you sleeping with my Aunt Emma?"

I thought I was going to go through the floor. I had completely forgotten that Mrs. Emma Winston was Marshall's aunt — his favorite aunt. She spoiled him rotten. I didn't think he would be so protective of her though.

Marshall didn't flinch. He stared back at Mr. Johnson. We weren't sure what was going to happen. Finally, Mr. Johnson said, "Y'all get out. Get out right now."

We gathered our things and headed for the door. Marshall stood up, still staring at Mr. Johnson, and Mr. Johnson fired his glare back at him. I pulled Marshall by his coat sleeve, and he backed out of the room, never taking his eyes off Mr. Johnson.

When we got outside I asked, "What was that about?"

"I just wanna know. He comes by to see my parents and he's always talking about how bad and how slick Rev. Tremmel is. He never gives details. He just rambles. It gets old, man. And I don't like the way he looks at my Aunt Emma. I can't stand that snuff-dipping fool. So, I just decided to ask him some questions."

Dumb me. I thought Marshall was hanging out with us for the food. But I should have known that, like Mitchell, he thought long and deep, and when he came after you — whoa.

I remember that guy those two nearly destroyed at Eastern Park, and the way Marshall called out Mitchell on his bullshit Rhonda story. That was classic.

Of course the event spread through the church like wildfire. It was the hot topic for a week or two, and then some other trivial sensationalized drama took its place.

I told myself to be really careful the next time I invite Marshall to Mt. Sinai.

I felt sorry for Mr. Johnson. He looked embarrassed, but his face moved to anger and displayed a look like he wanted to strangle Marshall.

Although we're not with Ms. Sonya's class anymore, we talk to her regularly. Four years with her was hardly enough, but change is inevitable. She's one of the few people who takes the time to listen to how we teenagers feel and what we're dealing with, which is such a contrast to what we have with Mr. Johnson.

But something is up with Ms. Sonya. That bubbly, comforting, nurturing woman has lost something. She still makes herself available and listens to us, but she doesn't hang around much after church. Even when she does mingle with the congregation following the service, part of her is in another dimension.

Her beauty has waned just a bit, but it's not from age or being unkempt. I'm not sure what it is. The brightness isn't there. She looks tired, drained. Her brown eyes are weak and troubled.

Rev. Tremmel continues his work. Sometimes he and Ms. Sonya ride to church together, but if he has engagements or appointments after service, she drives her 1972 medium blue metallic Gran Torino.

My boys and I love that car.

Rev. Tremmel has not only brought the church into the present, but he's also made connections with local colleges for tutoring, and created opportunities for folks to volunteer at the homeless shelter, hospital, and clinic. The man's constantly on the go. He's everywhere. He tells us about the conferences he attends, the business meetings, and other trips.

"All for the good of the church," he says.

"Remember, Tremmel rhymes with Grimmel, and this is where I'm supposed to be."

I understand being on the go, but it would be nice if he'd stop long enough to pay me my money. I know you're busy, but c'mon Rev. Tremmel.

The deacon board, Associate Minister Roger Faircloth, and others help when he's away.

While Rev. Tremmel's all over the place, Ms. Sonya seems to be getting worse. She converses and interacts with folks, but there's no depth. The distance continues to grow. It's forced and stiff. It's like she's going through the motions.

This Sunday after church I approach her as she walks to her car. Before I get my mind and mouth in sync, the question "What's the matter, Ms. Sonya?" leaps from my lips.

As she turns to respond, she can tell that I know she's not okay. She tilts her head, smiles weakly and says, "Thank you so much for asking, Mason, but I'm okay. I just have a lot on my mind."

As she utters these half-truths, her voice cracks with emotion. Her eyes well with tears, yet she continues to smile and hold fast to her proclamations and composure.

I think back to Rhonda's meltdown.

Although Ms. Sonya doesn't meltdown, I'm more convinced of how much she and Rhonda are alike. I desperately want to help her as much as I want to help Rhonda, but I'm not sure what to do for either of them.

Ms. Sonya and I know that what she says isn't true, but we also know that she can't share whatever's happening with me — at least not now.

I reluctantly accept her response, say good-bye, and wish her a good day.

As I start to walk away, she wraps her arms around me and gives me the tightest hug. It's not like the ones she's given before. It feels like a cry for help from a place deep within her.

She lets go and slides into the driver's seat. I wave to her, perplexed at what just happened. I want to tell her that her husband owes me fifty bucks, but now's not the time.

CHAPTER SEVEN

Marshall is the first of our group to get his driver license. What a proud day for him. Damn, I'm jealous.

Having a driver license is a precious coveted dimension of teenage freedom. As far as we're concerned, Marshall's now emancipated and we'll get our freedom through him. On top of that, because his folks have done well with their bakery business, they give him a car — a 1974 honey gold, Dodge Challenger with black interior and an AM/FM radio with an 8-track tape player. This ride is clean. It doesn't matter to us what kind of car it is. We're just glad our boy got one.

Marshall got his license on the first Friday in December, and his parents are letting him loose. They know he's a good driver and responsible. Hey, he's been driving the family's bakery truck illegally for years and has never been caught.

Of course the first thing we have to do is go cruising, so we gather at our scheduled time at Marshall's house.

We pile in the Challenger for the maiden voyage. It's a 45-minute drive to get to a major city from Grimmel, so we tool around town hoping somebody will see us in *our* new car. Wouldn't you know it — we don't see a soul — at least nobody that matters to us. No girls to flirt with, no guys to make jealous — nobody. We ride through the local parks, swing by Grimmel High School, cruise the hangout strips — nothing.

Where's everybody?

"Y'all want to go to Dirty Harry's?" Marshall asks.

I swear Marshall can eat anytime of the day or night. Where does it go? I think to myself, I wonder if we'll see Mr. Johnson getting an order for him and Mrs. Winston. For our sake, I hope Marshall doesn't see him.

The consensus is yes. I can't remember a time we all turned down food — especially fast food.

"Y'all got money?" Link asks.

"Yeah. The question is, 'Do *you* have money'" Dep fires back.

"I bet I got more money than you."

"Man, please. You so broke you can't even pay attention."

Here we go with the jokes again. Gotta love these guys.

Two cars are ahead of us in Dirty Harry's drive thru. The name epitomizes the spot. The red cursive lettering on the tall rectangle sign just off the road is badly faded. Six holes near the bottom from rocks thrown by hooligans expose fluorescent lights. The front windows are streaky and have large gray circles of film from being washed with dirty rags. This has to be one of the nastiest looking places to eat I've ever seen in my life, but the food is so good.

"Y'all got it together? You know what you want?" Marshall asks, as he stops the Challenger just short of the speaker.

"Man, you know they ain't got nothing but hamburgers and hot dogs, Mitchell says.

"That's just what we get all the time. They got other stuff. Y'all know what you want?"

"Yeah. Pull up," Dep says.

With surprising precision, we place our order.

In no time the clerk hands Marshall five white bags. Orange and brown grease stains decorate the bottoms. Onions, chili, toasted buns, and hot fries fill the car with their aroma. A tray of soft drinks follows.

She concludes the transaction filling Marshall's hands with extra napkins, straws, and change.

"Thank you," Marshall says. He passes the change back to Mitchell to distribute. He makes a right out of the parking lot. The car is quiet with the exception of opening bags and satiating moans.

"Damn. I told them I didn't want no pickles. Anybody want my pickles?" Link asks.

"Pass 'em over here," Dep says.

"Don't y'all get nothin' on my seats." Marshall says. "Especially you Dep, with yo' sloppy ass."

"Man, go head. Ain't nobody gon' git nothin' on yo' precious seats. Just turn yo' long head around and drive. Fool get a car and look at him. Think we supposed bow down. Make me sick."

Marshall's pissed.

"Boy, I'll — "

"You ain't gon' do —

"Stop y'all. Stop," Link says. "Just stop. Y'all givin' me headache. Let me enjoy my food."

Silence fills the car, as we all turn our attention to the job at hand — throwing down on our feast.

We decide to head home, but to avoid getting there too soon, Marshall goes the long way.

I look out the front passenger window and realize that we'll pass Rhonda's house. We're soon rounding "Manny's Curve," so her place will be on the right between the vacant lot and Mrs. Lane's old farm.

Large oak trees frame the white house, as it sits off the road. Neighbors in this area aren't very close to each other. Rhonda said her mom likes it this way.

"The distance between the houses helps keep people out of your business," she says.

I position myself so I can get a good look. I might get lucky, and she'll be outside.

We get to the bend, and I can see her driveway. There's a car there — Rev. Tremmel's Monte Carlo? That's odd.

It's 6:30 p.m. on a Friday. Rev. Tremmel always brags that when he's in town, Friday night is date night for Sonya and him. He's told the congregation many times, "If you can help it, don't call me on Fridays. Me and Sonya got business to take care of."

So, what's he doing there?

I hope everything's okay with Rhonda and Ms. Franks.

The guys are still eating and talking about how bad Grimmel's boys' basketball team is. They don't seem to notice where we are. If they do, they're not saying anything out loud.

"They pitiful. Marshall, I don't know why you don't play for the school, man. Can't nobody on the team beat you," Dep says.

"I know. But they got too many rules."

Mitchell sucks some root beer through his straw, opens his mouth and rips the loudest, deepest belch. Damn near rattles the car's windows.

"Man, I can smell everything you had to eat today up here. That's nasty." I say.

"I know, but it's better out than in."

I shake my head and put the rest of my burger in the bag.

***

The next weekend we decide to cruise again. There's a dance this Friday night at Grimmel High and rumor has it there's also a house party on Angel Street. We've got to grace both places with our presence.

Going out for us is sort of a big deal. None of us are high on the teenage social ladder, but we aren't at the bottom. We really don't care because we know we're gonna be cleaner than the board of health when we step out.

It's comical and fascinating to see our approaches to fashion when it's time to party. We've got our distinct ways of dressing and hairstyles. Afros are fading, but we all still wear medium length hair.

Dep's got some curls, which the ladies love. I sport my teeny weenie Afro. It hasn't changed much at all for a while, but I can at least manage to get it even.

Mitchell is the king of putting a part in any hairstyle. That brother will put a part down middle, on the side, up high, down low, or at an angle. He can work a part.

Marshall's the most creative when it comes to hair. Besides his family being in the bakery business, his older sister has a beauty shop on Main Street a few blocks from our house. Consequently, this brother has 1001 hairstyles. Conked, straight, Afro, you name it.

Tonight, he's wearing what we nicknamed the "Duke Ellington." His sister permed his hair, and he combed it straight back. It stops at the base of his neck. She freshened it up a bit and made it extra shiny. Of course we're clowning him, but it didn't matter. This long tall joker can wear anything, including this hairstyle, with so much confidence. He makes it all work for him.

Our "going out" jeans have hard pressed creases from hours of ironing and loads of starch. Our shirts are crisp and razor sharp.

After some work with white shoe polish and a toothbrush, our sneakers gleam.

We bathe in cheap cologne. The strength and mixing of fragrances is enough to choke a horse. But we've got to look and smell good in order to feel good.

Five fresh, clean, and "dressed to the nines" brothers hop in the Challenger, chomping at the bit to start the night. The game plan is to hit the high school dance first. If it's happening, stay there for a while. Then hit the Angel Street house party.

We have until midnight to do any and all damage.

High school dances in Grimmel are either light or dark. Light means that the DJ is white, so the music will be "white" — rock, pop, with sprinkles of popular R&B. A dark dance means the opposite — mostly black folks, a black DJ, and lots of R&B and Funk. We don't know what kind of dance it'll be, so we have to go to find out.

We pull up in front of the school.

"There's Frank Harden," Dep says. "Ask him what's going on."

Marshall calls him over.

Frank's an older guy that hangs around high school dances. He's not drunk — yet, but he's tipsy. The "X" on the back of his left hand from a yellow fluorescent marker tells us he's been inside and can give us the scoop.

"What's happening, Frank?" Marshall asks. "You been inside?"

"Yeah man. It's bout half and half in there," he says.

Well, It looks like we have a new category — a grey dance.

"I'm 'bout to go back in. Just came out to get me a taste."

He looks the car over and gives an admiring head nod.

Frank lifts the paper cup in his right hand and points it toward the auditorium.

"See that lil' white girl peepin' at me through the window?"

We look. There's six white girls looking out of the window — none of them are looking at Frank.

Marshall humors him. "Yeah, I see."

He slaps Marshall's hand.

"You know what I'm bout to do."

"Nothing," Mitchell mumbles.

"All right man. Do yo' thang." Marshall says.

Frank throws a black power fist to us and strolls on wobbly legs back toward the entrance of the school.

"That fool goin' to jail," Mitchell says. "What is Frank? 30 years old? Them girls he's talkin' about are barely in high school. And they sho' as hell don't want nothing to do with his ol' drunk ass."

We park, take a last look at ourselves in the Challenger side mirrors and pimp walk our way up to the entrance, doing our best to be cool, being careful not to scuff up our shoes, giving the obligatory brother nod to guys lined along the sidewalk.

The crowd outside is peppered with folks sipping concealed homemade mixed drinks, cheap wine, and beer from white Styrofoam cups, puffing on cigarettes, and guys constructing intricate plans to get next to somebody's daughter.

When we get to the entrance, we hear the DJ playing an unheard mix of pop, R&B and Funk. We're taken aback because this has never happened. After a quick conference meeting and vote, we decide to pay the two-dollar cover and see what's happening.

Familiar faces pack the auditorium. Many of them we see five days a week, but there're people from surrounding schools as well. It's funny how one can tell almost immediately when someone isn't from your area.

I'm nodding my head to the beat. The atmosphere feels good.

But not good enough for me to ask anybody to dance. I don't want that rejection tonight.

I've been to lots of dances, and the results have been the same. Politely ask a girl to dance — fast or slow — and receive a vehement "no," an obligatory fake smile and turning of the head — that means you have been dismissed. There's also the embarrassing "walk away." That's when the girl walks away while you're still asking your question — or the even more humiliating, "not right now," and then some clown that looks like he could kick the principle's ass or has children my age, comes up and asks her right after you. She nearly breaks her neck running to the dance floor with that fool.

That's my reality.

Who knows? Maybe I will get up the courage to ask somebody to dance before we leave.

We continue to play our cool role, standing in the back of the auditorium, holding up the wall, perusing the sea of people, and soaking in the vibes. The music mix is working. Non-dancing folks bob their heads and pat their feet. Those on the dance floor enjoy themselves. I think we might be here for a bit.

I'm starting to have this strange feeling. It's hard to describe. It's not like someone's watching you, but it sort of feels that way. It makes me look around, but nothing seems out of the ordinary.

Our group has another board meeting and votes to stay at the dance for a while longer. We'll split up and meet in front of the school when the dance shuts down at 11 p.m.

I meander through the crowd, nodding, smiling, avoiding unnecessary contact, evaluating fashion, passively analyzing colognes, perfumes and in some cases — unadulterated funk. I find a seat along the wall near the exit. It's a great spot. I can see nearly the entire room.

There's loud mouth Jake talking to some girl. You can hear that boy three miles away. Her ears are probably bleeding.

Oh Lord, there's mud mouth Marilyn. She's a cute girl, but her teeth look like she's been sucking rocks and dirt through a straw.

I see blabbermouth Brenda, Grimmel High's Gossip queen. If you want something told or an event publicized for free, BB is your girl.

There's overgrown Oscar. When we were in the fifth grade I swear this man-boy bully was six feet tall and had a moustache and Afros growing under his arms. No wonder he was so mean. I got so sick of that boy picking on us.

When we were little, Link and I lit Oscar's ass up in Ms. Sonya's class. He couldn't say words that started with 'str.' They always came out 'skr.' We set him up so he had to read the word "straw." When it came out "skraw," we and the rest of the class almost peed on ourselves.

Wait a minute. That can't be. Is that Rhonda? I just know my eyes and mind are playing tricks on me. It *is* her. She's standing about 30-feet across from me, next to one of the light switches, just opposite the storage closets. I don't think she's seen me, so I quickly blend in with the crowd.

I can still see her. She's also perusing the room and occasionally looking down at her watch. Should I go over? What should I say? Should I ask her to dance? Is my breath okay?

I slip out to the bathroom — nose, eyes okay, breath okay. Pop a mint just in case. Brush off my clothes. Swallow. Exhale.

I decide I'm going to say something to her.

The room grows two sizes larger and my feet turn to stone. I head over to where she is, but it feels like it's taking forever to get there.

I keep trying to talk myself into playing it safe and making a hasty retreat before it's too late. But I keep putting one foot in front of the other.

I get closer and realize that she's talking to Peggy.

Peggy spots me first and waves.

Peggy and I are cool. We had French together a couple of years back. I know that she knew Rhonda away from school, so it's not a complete surprise to see them together.

Rhonda looks up when Peggy waves. She smiles and mouths, "Hi."

The music isn't too loud, but you have to listen hard and get fairly close to the person to hear very well.

We exchange pleasantries the best we can through the music.

I see Rhonda's lips ask, "Are you having a good time?"

I nod yes and ask them the same question. Both nod affirmatively, and then there's that awkward silence in the midst of the booming music. All three of us nervously look in different directions around the room, glance at each other, exchange uncomfortable smiles, and search the floor for what to do or say next.

I take this as my cue to leave. As I wave good-bye and start my retreat, Rhonda touches my elbow and asks, "Are you leaving? I hope not. I want to talk to you."

I wasn't sure if I heard her correctly, but I said "okay," hoping I had.

"Do you want to go outside?" she asks.

My head nods yes, before I realize I'd done so. She whispers something to Peggy and starts toward the exit. I wave at Peggy and follow her.

We make our way toward the auditorium glass doors through the dance floor heat and writhing bodies, and welcome the cool night air. It's a crisp evening. Not too cold.

Through the branches and remaining oak and maple leaves I gaze briefly at the stars decorating the black sky with their brilliance. Although these things go unnoticed for the most part, they set the perfect atmosphere for this impromptu summit with Rhonda.

I spot an empty wooden bench just beyond the administration building. The streetlamp by the school's entrance illuminates the way and provides just enough light to see each other faces.

"Have a seat," I say, motioning to the bench after brushing it off. "How are you doing?"

"I'm okay. I wanted to apologize for my behavior and the distance I've put between us the last couple of months. I'm really sorry you had to deal with that."

"No apology necessary. We all have our moments."

I feel awkward talking about what happened, so I quickly change the subject.

"You and Peggy hang out much?"

"Not really. We've been in classes together and got to know each other. We talk on the phone sometimes. Our mothers know each other too. You know she lives way over on Conner Road, so we don't see each other too often outside of school. I just had to get out of the house tonight. Peggy called, so here I am."

I listen intently, trying to catch and savor every word because she's actually talking to me. I mean *talking* to me about something other than school project stuff.

Rhonda's revealing a lot. I can sense that at the moment she finally feels comfortable enough with me to let me in a little bit.

We go on for a few minutes chatting about mundane subjects that of course are fascinating to me because I'm talking about them with Rhonda.

As we talk, I remember that she said she wanted to speak with me about something. I'm anxious to know what it is but I don't want to press the issue or disrupt our priceless exchange. I'm determined to let her make the transition if and when she wants to.

"I really want to apologize for that day I broke down," she says.

"Really, Rhonda. It was no problem."

"But — it's more. It's more than you know. You don't understand why I was that way."

Okay. *This* is what she wants to talk about. I get it now.

She pauses and looks towards the sky. Her well-manicured fingernails gently tap her knees through her tight-fitting designer jeans.

Through the streetlamp's pale blue-green light I see Rhonda turn and look directly at me. Her eyes are clear and focused. Her face somber and still.

Just above a whisper she says, "Can I trust you?"

"Sure," I replied, afraid of where the conversation was going and where she might be taking me.

"I mean really. Can I trust you?" Her eyes don't move. I feel them probe my face for truth and loyalty. Her expression remains stoic, serious.

"Yes, Rhonda you can." I do my best to ensure her that I'm as honorable and trustworthy as they come.

She pauses again, looking down at the ground, as if gathering momentum to verbally fling this perplexing matter my way.

"There's something going on at my house that's not right. It's been happening for a long time. I've been dealing with it. I've never told anyone. But it's getting so hard to keep it together. I feel like I'm going crazy."

Her eyes begin to water a bit. Her voice is firm but not far from cracking. Her hands are now becoming clenched fists. She uses an analogy from some of the Black literature we've been studying.

"It's like I'm enslaved with invisible chains and I can't find a way to break them. Do you know what I mean?"

I don't. But I feel I have to try to make some connection or at least make her think that I understand.

"Uh, yeah, I think so. Uh, it's kind of like when your parents put some heavy punishment on you for something that really wasn't that serious. Yeah, yeah I know what you mean."

I didn't know what the hell I was talking about, but I did my best.

She knows that I don't completely get it, but she's gracious. She smiles.

"Sort of. It's a little more than that though. I'm trapped in a very difficult situation, and what makes it harder is that I'm not in it by myself. My mother and I are trying to figure out how to deal with this person — this — person who's terrorizing us. We're not sure what to do, but we've got to do something before it's too late. The other day he made us both — "

"Hey man. We gotta roll."

Damn. It's Dep.

"Marshall remembered he got to take his sister to work. You know she work the graveyard shift at the mill. He pauses quickly, and says, "Hey, Rhonda."

"Hi, Dep."

"Let's hit it man. He's starting to freak out 'cause he knows his sister will beat his ass if he makes her late again. She probably won't do his hair anymore."

"I'm coming."

Rhonda pats me on the shoulder and says, "Go. We'll talk soon. I promise"

Lord knows I don't want to go, but that's my ride, and it's too late and too far to walk, especially in the dark. I don't want to impose on Peggy to take me home. I know her, but I don't know her well enough to have her drive Rhonda and then make a special trip for me. Conner Road is no trip around the corner, so to take both of us would be too much. Rhonda knows this and is okay with the situation.

I really want to know right now what's happening with her, but I'll find out soon enough.

She stands next to the bench as I slowly walk backward towards the parking lot. I wave to her. From the distance I hear, "Man, bring yo' ass on." I turn and run to the car.

CHAPTER EIGHT

Daylight seeping through my cracked blinds pries at my eyelids. It's time to get up. Got stuff to do this Saturday. I'm still tingling and frustrated, but strangely happy. Last night, I talked to Rhonda, and she talked to me. And I was about to find out what's happening with her. That damn Dep.

This Saturday is going to be a long day. Mr. and Mrs. Neal are letting me work at the print shop from seven to ten this morning. That doesn't happen very often, so I take advantage — got to make that money.

I down a bowl of cereal and get dressed. It's early, but my youngest sister is already up watching cartoons. She never looks up, as I make my way out the backdoor.

The work Mr. Neal has for me today is easy, but time consuming. Sorting papers, correlating, and cleaning machines. It's monotonous, but makes the time go by fast.

After I leave the shop, I spend a few hours helping of all people — Mrs. Winston — clean out her attic and move furniture. I swear my mother will volunteer me for anything, but I'm grateful this time because Mrs. Winston said she's going to pay pretty well. I still don't like what she said to Link, and I keep getting images in my mind of her and Mr. Johnson — gag. But business is business.

We go back and forth in her bedrooms, moving various pieces of furniture. Some of this stuff is heavy. When we finish with this, we move to the attic. This lady is making me earn every penny.

Mrs. Winston's attic is for the most part surprisingly neat — boxes and books are stacked tidily largest to smallest, or leaned carefully against the walls. Because it was cool outside, the attic was comfortable. After shifting around some items, she asked me to pull down an old trunk and some of the boxes. Mrs. Winston stands at the bottom of the attic stairs, and I pass her the stuff she wants. Everything smells like mothballs. I hate that smell.

Mrs. Winston says, "Let's take a break." And I'm glad to. The work isn't hard, but I want to stop for a few minutes.

"Come in the kitchen." She disappears through swinging doors. I climb down the stairs and quickly make my way behind her.

Her kitchen is immaculate. Gleaming blue and white appliances and a shiny white tiled floor. And she's got cookies--chocolate chip, peanut butter, and sugar. Yes.

"Help yourself."

As I select my treats, she pulls a pitcher of lemonade from the fridge and pours a glass for me. My mouth waters a bit. This is just what I need.

"Here you go Mason."

"I think I'll have a little more myself," she says while topping off hers.

I turn my vessel up. And I spot a half empty fifth of gin by the sink. The top with its broken seal sits next to it.

I reach for another cookie and look closely at Mrs. Winston. She's twirling her glass, staring out the window smiling at nothing.

"Mrs. Winston, you okay?" I ask.

She turns and looks at me with the vacant grin still intact.

"I'm just fine."

Yep, she sure is. She's feeling just fine. Mrs. Winston is lit.

Earlier she kept going back and forth to the kitchen while I adjusted the boxes in the attic. I thought she was cooking something. Mrs. Winston was sipping.

"Let's go to the living room," she says. I grab my glass and snag a few more cookies.

She flops down in a green easy chair, never spilling a drop of her gin-lemonade mixture.

"Whew. I'm bushed," she says.

No, you're tipsy.

"Honey, wretch around that trunk and hand me that black box."

I carefully walk across the hardwood floor and pick it up. It's an old faded hatbox, but it has some weight to it.

"Careful," she says, as I pass it to her.

"Sit down. I want to show you something."

I slide a leather ottoman next to her and take a seat.

She blows the light layer of dust off the lid and lifts it slowly.

The box is full of pictures and knickknacks. Mrs. Winston smiles as she runs her fingers across some of the photos on top of the pile.

"Lord, child, I ain't seen these things in years."

I didn't recognize anybody in the pictures, so I make myself comfortable as I can as she reminisces.

"Look," she says, beckoning me to slide closer. "This is my husband, Johnny. God rest his soul."

I never knew Mr. Winston. He died awhile back. Handsome guy.

"That's nice," I say.

She keeps flipping and reflecting. And now I'm fighting to stay awake.

"You know who this is?" she asks, pointing at a figure in another black and white snapshot.

I have no clue. The picture is of two fine women dressed in puffed-sleeved blouses and tight pencil skirts that did them justice. One lady has her hand on her shapely hips, and the other leans casually against her friend, pulling her skirt up to show a beautifully toned thigh. Their faces are made up, and their hair is in victory rolls.

"Who's that?" I ask.

She laughs.

"That's me and Mrs. Potts."

"Who?" I ask before I realize what I'm saying.

Her laughing continues. "Me and Mrs. Potts — Link's grandmother."

I think to myself, ain't no way in h —

"Lord knows we don't look like that now, but we was sho' nuff hot stuff then."

She was telling the truth. They were hot stuff. I look at Mrs. Winston out of the corner of my eye and look back at the picture. Damn. I want to ask her if I can keep it, but I don't. I do my best to memorize it.

"Look. Who's that?" she asks, pushing another picture towards me.

I know this one.

"That's Mr. Potts."

"That's right."

He was sharp in his suit, sitting in a metal lawn chair in their front yard with his legs crossed.

"Well that's enough. Let's ..."

As Mrs. Winston gets up, she knocks the box over and pictures and trinkets go flying everywhere.

Mrs. Winston is definitely lubricated.

Instinctively, I kneel down and start picking up the items. She leans over from her seat and joins me.

Wow. That's a beautiful pocket watch. Silver with gold trim. The fall sent it under the corner of the easy chair, so I don't think she sees it. What is Mrs. Winston doing with that? I put it back in the box. She still doesn't see it.

I look back at the assorted sized photos. Most are of people I don't know from decades past. But I notice there are lots of pictures of Mrs. Winston and Mrs. Potts, many like the ones she showed me. There are pictures of Mr. and Mrs. Winston, Mr. and Mrs. Potts, but there's another attractive couple I didn't recognize. I stop gathering and focus on one of the photos of the mysterious, good-looking pair. It looks like they were at a fair or something.

"Who's this?" I ask.

Mrs. Winston leans over, looks at the picture and looks at me.

"Who does it look like?"

I study the photograph a little more.

"It kind of looks like Mr. Cleotis Johnson, but —"

"It is."

I'm floored. He looked incredible. Still slim. Neat. Dressed up. No nasty snuff smashed in his lower lip.

"But who's the woman?"

"That was his wife."

"What? He was married?" I ask, trying not to sound so surprised.

"Yes, he was. Might not look like it now, but Mr. Johnson was something else. The ladies loved Cleotis."

I wonder if we were talking about the same person.

"Didn't matter though. He was in love with Lois."

"Lois?"

"Yes, Lois. They met in New York. We used to have some good times then."

"Lois was his — ?"

"Yes, Lois was his wife. It's funny. She was from Grimmel, but her family left when she was a little girl. Moved to Maryland I believe. She and Johnson met while he was in the army in the early '40s. Got married real fast — like four months. Said they was in love. Hmpf. I think that heifer was pregnant. Potts and I tried to tell Johnson Lois won't no good, but his nose was wide open."

"What happened?"

"I told you she won't no good. She had the baby — a little boy — cute lil' thing. Johnson was crazy about that boy. But that heifer left Johnson for some slick-talking fool she met in New York. And she took the baby. That damn near killed Johnson. He tried to find them, but it was like they disappeared. Last thing I heard was somebody shot and killed her and her boyfriend. Don't know what happened to the baby."

Wow. I don't know what to say. I'll never look at Mr. Johnson the same.

"What was the baby's name?"

"You know what? I don't know if I ever knew for sure. But they used to call him 'Moonbeam' because he was so light."

For some reason, I don't think Mrs. Winston is telling me everything. But why should she?

She shows me more pictures, but my mind is flooded with what she told me happened to Mr. Johnson. I can't imagine losing my wife to another man and my only child too? I'm surprised he hasn't killed somebody.

I focus on more of the pictures. There's something eerie about some of them, but I don't know what it is.

I notice that the room has become awfully quiet and still. I quickly learn why. Mrs. Winston is out. Her head is nestled on the back of the chair. Mouth open. Glasses askew. Light snoring has commenced. I take her half-empty glass and put it on the side table. The handmade quilt from the back of the couch I lay over her covers her legs to her shoulders. I fold it neatly just under her neck.

The watch is peeking from between the piles of photos. It's like it's calling me. I pick it up and find a clasp. After a little struggle, but I manage to open it. An intriguing picture sits inside.

I freeze when Mrs. Potts unexpectedly snorts and adjusts her head. But she remains comatose.

I stuff the watch and some photographs in my jacket pocket, slip quietly out of her front door and head home. I'm sure Mrs. Winston won't mind me borrowing these things. I'll bring everything back soon.

CHAPTER NINE

Sunday morning comes fast. I'm a little sore from carrying boxes of clothes and moving furniture for Mrs. Winston, but I'm still somewhat in shock from what she told me about Mr. Johnson. Shock, sore body and all, I still have to make it to church or my mother won't shut up. To get out of going I try the standard excuses, "I don't feel like going this morning. I'm tired."

"Oh you're goin," my mom says. "Ain't nothing wrong with you. You gotta sing this morning."

"But —"

"But nothing. Boy, get up and get dressed."

My father passes my doorway, stops and looks at me with a sarcastic grin and shakes his head. He knows how bad I don't want to go, but we both understand that this is a battle he can't fight, and I can't win.

I surrender and swing my feet onto the lukewarm floor.

***

Being in the choir stand gives me a bird's eye view of the congregation. With the exception of the front of the pulpit because we're behind it, I can see everything — the deacons, deaconesses, ushers, and even my sisters and their friends sneaking out to make a mad dash to the convenience store up the hill to get treats before church service starts.

Everything and everybody are in their usual places, but I sense some strangeness in the air.

Man, we sound some kind of good this Sunday morning. I'm really not one for choirs and singing, but it's another one of those things my mother "asked" us to do. It's okay at times, but when Mrs. Wilcox, the young adult choir director, has her ass on her shoulders, rehearsals are long and boring. This morning the work we put in paid off though. We just destroyed the congregation with a smoking rendition of the Hawkins "Oh Happy Day."

Before Rev. Tremmel speaks, he turns around and smiles big at us — his stamp of approval — something that we all wait to see when we've finish singing. We smile back, knowing that we've done our job — well.

He grabs the energy from the song and launches hard into his message.

I study the audience.

Associate Minster Roger Faircloth sits to Tremmel's left, leaning in as if to catch every word falling from his mouth and enthusiastically "encourages" him.

"Preach it pastor. That's right. They need to hear that. Say it again."

Faircloth is such a suck up. He wants to be the assistant pastor so bad he'll do or say almost anything. He's buried deep in Rev. Tremmel's butt.

The deacons are to my left in their assigned section in the pulpit, Mr. Percy Stockton, Mr. Lawrence Mitchell, my main man, Mr. Cleotis Johnson, and Mr. Preston Faircloth, brother of the brownnoser.

The deaconesses are on the opposite end, Mrs. Fannie Mae Jackson, Mrs. Lula Carrington, Mrs. Betty Lee Richmond, and Ms. Sonya Tremmel.

Ms. Sonya stands out like a red rose among wilting daisies. She's decades younger than all of them, and nothing against the other women, but even with whatever she's going through, Ms. Sonya is still strikingly beautiful.

I keep my eye on her because of the exchange we had before. I shoot brief glances her way. She, like everyone else, watches her husband and listens intensely. She smiles. She nods with the rest of the congregation. She responds to his words. But it's not like before.

I've sat in the choir stand many times and seen Ms. Sonya energetically support her husband as he preached. She's not vocal, but you can sense her energy, support, and assurance.

Today's something else. She sits in the same place, but it's as if she's going through the motions — kind of mimicking what everybody else is doing. At times I could have sworn that she looked away — rolling her eyes. Then again, maybe it's me. There have been times I thought I saw things that weren't there, and this could be the case. Maybe I'm looking at her through our last conversation in the parking lot. I can't see Rev. Tremmel's face, but he seems to be unfazed.

Following the benediction, we sing the seven-fold Amen.

Everyone mingles.

I continue to watch Ms. Sonya.

She shakes hands, gives hugs and kisses as usual, but one thing is different. She never makes her way to Rev. Tremmel. Every time, and I mean every time Rev. Tremmel preaches, at some point afterwards, Ms. Sonya goes to him and kisses him on the cheek — a ritual that confirms her support and seems to publically solidify their relationship.

This Sunday, after she puts down Alice Rose's baby, she makes her way through the side exit.

I unzip my choir robe, throw it over my shoulder, and dash to the fellowship hall. In a second, I hang up the vestment, grab my jacket and make a B-line to the parking lot to look for Ms. Sonya. I see her heading for her Torino. She and Rev. Tremmel have driven separately again.

I start walking towards her, but I hear Deacon Preston Lee calling me.

"Mason, hold on a second."

I wait for him.

He and his mahogany cane make their way to me — *click, tap, click, tap.* The metal taps on his shoes and his cane create a distinct rhythm.

I'm close enough to Ms. Sonya to speak, and I do. She turns and smiles, continuing to put her belongings in order to go in her car.

Although it's December, it's still unseasonably warm. It's one of those days the old folks say you can catch "the P-neumonia" because it's cold enough for a coat in the morning but too hot for it by the afternoon.

The weather victimized Ms. Sonya. It's now too warm for the big brown overcoat she's wearing.

Deacon Lee throws his arm around my shoulders.

"Y'all sang this mornin' boy. I mean y'all was singin' up something.

I hear him, but I watch Ms. Sonya open her car door to put her things in the backseat.

Deacon Lee finishes doling out his compliments, pats me on the shoulder, and he and his cane walk in the opposite direction.

I look up and notice that the jacket sleeves from her beige pantsuit come off when she removes her overcoat. The sleeveless lavender blouse exposes her left arm.

Deep purple and dark blue bruises run around her triceps and bicep. She quickly adjusts the jacket and slides off her overcoat, looking around to see if anyone has witnessed her markings. I quickly kneel down pretending to tie my shoe.

Ms. Sonya's bruises take me back to a precarious situation a few years ago.

The Rogers family lived next door to us. They were very similar to us — three girls ranging from six to twelve, and one boy, thirteen. We played with the children, and my parents sometimes played Bid Whist and Pinochle with their parents. Their father, Herman Rogers, was a piece of work. This cat was nickel slick.

Mr. Rogers was a tall, fair-skinned, handsome man. I'd heard mothers and girls in the neighborhood talk about how good-looking he was. But he had a horrible reputation of seducing and sleeping with women he wasn't married to.

I didn't like him because he was pretentious and phony. I didn't trust him. And the rumors of his extracurricular activity felt true to me.

He really needed to be careful because his wife, Rita Rogers, was rather fine. She was petite with a shapely figure and girlish face. Her shoulder length hair had been dyed reddish-blond, and it meshed with her sienna complexion. Her light brown eyes pulled everything together. Not that he could do much about it, but Mitchell had a huge crush on her. He was just a teenager, but the look in his eye when Mrs. Rogers came around was beyond lustful. I understood his feelings to some degree, but Mitchell had it bad.

I'm sure Mrs. Rogers had her fair share of suitors, catcalls, and offers. But as far as we knew, she was deeply faithful to her husband.

God only knows why.

One spring Friday night while our family watched the usual network television line up, we heard loud crashes and screams coming from the Rogers' house. My mom opened the front door to see what was happening, and a blur, nearly knocking her down, bolted through the living room, ran down our hall, into our bathroom. We heard the door slam followed by the turning of the lock.

It was Mrs. Rogers.

"He's trying to kill me. He's trying to kill me." she yelled.

My father calmly got up from his recliner and placed his beer on the living room table. My sisters and I didn't know what to think or do. My mom talked to Mrs. Rogers through the bathroom door trying to calm her down and figure out what was happening.

"Rita, what's goin' on?" My mom asked.

"He crazy. He crazy. He's trying to kill me. Please don't let him in here."

The Rogers' children were standing in our front yard screaming and crying hysterically, "Daddy crazy. He got a gun. He trying to kill our mama."

Unfazed, my father said to my mother, "Call the police."

He had an expression and demeanor I'd never seen before. He was too calm. He walked out of the front door towards the Rogers' house.

Fear quickly grew inside me and I ran after him not knowing what he was going to do. Without breaking stride he turned his head to the right and yelled at me out of the side of his mouth, "Go back."

I stopped in my tracks. I couldn't go back, so I watched from that spot.

When he got to their front door he called for Mr. Rogers.

"Herman." His voice was stern.

Rogers came out screaming and cursing, waving a .45 in his right hand.

My father didn't move. Very calmly he said, "Did you hit Rita?"

"Yeah, nigga. I smacked that stupid ass bitch, and when I catch her, I'll beat her ass ag — ."

Before he could get the last word off his tongue, my father snatched Mr. Roger's right wrist, which caused him to drop the gun. He crushed his right knee with a thundering stomp, and in a flash, pinned him face down to the cement porch. With a quick swoop, he flung the gun into the yard. He twisted Mr. Rogers' right arm so hard behind his back, I swore he was going to rip it off.

"If you don't hold still I'll break it. So help me. Don't move."

The police station is less than a mile away. Soon their sirens screamed in the distance growing louder by the second.

My father continued to hold down Mr. Rogers. His knee pushed hard in his back. Once he was still, my father, still twisting Rogers' arm, bent down a few inches from his ear and delivered a message that shocked me.

"Listen to me, you weak ass son of a bitch. If you ever hit that woman again, I'll kill you. Do you understand me?"

There was silence.

"I said, do you understand me?"

Mr. Rogers managed to slide a muffled "Yes" from his lips mashed against the porch.

By the time the police arrived, everyone in the neighborhood had gathered in and around the Rogers' yard. Some were concerned. Others were just nosey — looking for a story to exploit.

Two officers jumped on the porch and took over my father's position. He explained what happened. Rogers offered no opposition.

"And make sure you get that .45 over there in the grass," my father said, as he headed back home.

"Careful. It's loaded." he added.

Mrs. Rogers emerged from our house. Her face bloodied and swollen. Cuts were open on both lips. She held a white hand towel with ice over her left eye. The Rogers children clung to her, still crying and sobbing, but grateful their mother was alive.

Why did Mr. Rogers do this?

Mrs. Rogers told my mother that she confronted Herman about one of his extramarital affairs, and he went crazy. He told her that it was none of her business and he was going to teach her a lesson for "messing" in his business. He dragged her in the bathroom, closed the door, and beat her, hitting her in the stomach and ribs knocking the wind out of her.

Then he went to work on her face, snatching the .45 from his waistband and pistol-whipping her. She said she got out when he swung hard at her head, and she ducked. He missed, tripped over the rug, fell into the shower curtain, and landed in the tub. She dashed through the door and took off for the first safe place she could get to.

The police arrested Mr. Rogers and tossed him in rear of the cruiser. Flashing blue lights bounced off the crowd, trees, and houses as they spoke with my parents and Mrs. Rogers.

We heard tires screeching on the road and a '72 beige Buick LeSabre roared into our driveway. It was Mrs. Rogers' sister Pinky. She jumped out of her car, ran straight to her sister, and threw her arms around her.

During the embrace, Pinky looked up in time to see the police car making the left turn out of the driveway. Mr.

Rogers strained his neck looking out of the rear-view window. He and Pinky locked eyes. She flipped her middle finger at him.

With the exception of my father's heroic act, I didn't think we'd done anything much, but the Rogers' family was extremely thankful. We didn't know this was not the first time until Mrs. Rogers told us. After they gathered themselves and some personal items, Pinky took them to stay with her for the night.

My father came outside, sat down on the porch and placed his can of beer next to him.

"Come here," he said to me. I sat next to him, the can separated us.

As we watched the crowed disperse, he said, "Son, that's not a man. It takes a coward to beat a woman. I couldn't stand by and let that happen. I don't like to get in people's business, but I can't let stuff like that go. He's lucky I didn't break his arm or worse. I hope you never see anything like that again, but I wanted you to know why I did what I did. You understand?"

"Yes, sir."

I was proud and scared. Scared that my father could have been shot. Proud that he stepped in to do something.

By the following Tuesday, the Rogers' house was empty and the family was gone. We learned that Mrs. Rogers divorced Herman and moved out of state. We didn't know for sure, but the word on the street was that Mr. Rogers received a number of threats on his life from her family and several friends. He too left the area — maybe to save his life.

That incident did something to me. Even though my father and I talked about it, I couldn't wrap my head around why a man would beat a woman like that. Sure, I've seen my parents argue, but my father never struck my mother, nor did she hit him — no matter how upset they were.

I understand better why my parents tried to teach me that lesson. I can't strike my sisters under any circumstances. Lord knows I want to sometimes. But after seeing the violence this punk Mr. Rogers inflicted and the talk with my father, I vowed that I would never stand for a man hitting a woman. I didn't know what I'd do, but I wasn't going to stand for it.

Recalling what happened with Mrs. Rogers, I know without question how those bruises on Ms. Sonya's arm got there. But could Rev. Tremmel ever do anything like that?

I'm not sure what to do, but I know what I saw. In some ways, I wish someone else saw her arm because I'm not sure what my level of responsibility is or what I should do. But I know someone has hurt Ms. Sonya.

I go back and forth whether to say something and if so, to whom.

I decide to talk to Link.

Link and I agreed to watch today's football game.

I'm into the NFL, but I don't have a team that I route for all the time. My dad's an Atlanta Falcons fan, so I have some fondness for them. I often pull for the underdog, so today I'm pulling for Atlanta. They're playing the Dallas Cowboys.

Link's a big Dallas fan. That's tough because although I don't have a favorite team per se — I hate Dallas.

Of course they massacre the Falcons. Damn. Now I have to listen to Link the rest of the day tell me the ins and outs of why the Cowboys are the best NFL franchise.

After the game, we sit on the edge of my porch and tease my sister's orange tabby kitten with some yellow string.

Even though Dallas beat Atlanta "like they stole something," Link is gracious. He only talks trash for about a half hour after the game.

Finally, I dive into the deep end.

"Hey, man, do you think Ms. Sonya's okay?" Link thinks for minute.

"I guess so. She's still fine, if that's what you mean."

"No — I mean — yeah. She's still fine, but she doesn't seem to be herself, maybe a little sad."

"Why do you say that?"

"I don't know. When I watch her sometimes, she looks like she's struggling to make it through the day. Like she's just going through the motions."

"Well, now that you mention it, she doesn't really say as much as she used to. She used to speak to me after church every Sunday. The past couple of months she just smiled and kept going. I hadn't thought too much about it, but — "

"Look, Link, you my boy and I want to tell you something. I trust you cause you've never lied to me or told any secrets I've told you."

"Okay, man." he says. "You sound serious. What's happening?"

I tell him about what I saw on Ms. Sonya's arm. Link sits in silence, looking blankly at the kitten exerting all of her young prowess to capture the dangling string. After a few seconds he responds, "Interesting. Interesting."

CHAPTER TEN

The weather's still unseasonably warm, but it's starting to feel like Christmas. Assorted sizes of plastic Santa Clauses, holly wreathes with red berries and miscellaneous styles of Christmas trees decorate windows, yards, and front doors. Street lamps in downtown Grimmel wear their special holiday outfits made of ringing bells and angels blowing trumpets.

The big white southern Baptist church on Maple Street has started their annual live nativity scene. This takes place at night during the week of Christmas. My French teacher, Ms. Baker, plays the part of Mary. We go by and make sure she sees us. Maybe it'll earn us some extra credit.

It's that time of year when nativity scenes appear throughout Grimmel along with all kinds of tasteful and gaudy decorations. There's something fascinating about watching people "act out" the nativity story. I wouldn't do it, but it's entertaining watching somebody else.

One house in particular goes over board when it comes to decoration. The story is that some guy who owns a small white rambler just off Cline Street and Oak Avenue loves to decorate for Christmas. He lives alone, never married, and doesn't have any children. But he loves Christmas. So he spends months covering every inch of his house, trees, and bushes with colored lights. His yard contains every piece of Christmas paraphernalia you can imagine. His finished product is grotesque, garish, and charming, and a long standing tradition in Grimmel.

Once the sun goes down, cars line up on Cline Street to catch a glimpse of his house. Every year our family follows suit. We pile in the station wagon and join the masses to gawk and be amazed. In a small town like ours, rituals and traditions like this blur racial and religious lines and create a sense of harmony — if only for a little while.

Mt. Sinai also has a tradition of putting on a Christmas program that consists of a play preceded by children giving speeches. I'm not a fan of participating, but of course this was another one of those things you can't say no to.

Ms. Sonya directs the programs along with some help from a few parents, and they're always a success. There's something about children dressing up and saying speeches and singing Christmas carols off key that's absolutely adorable. It doesn't matter how good or bad they are. It's always fun.

My sisters and I are big contributors to the programs because there's so many of us. Since we could speak we've been a part of the annual stage production — the one to three line speeches and the full paragraphs with hand gestures, make decorations, and sing songs. I've been in the Christmas plays for a few years, and my sisters are following suit.

Graduating from high school brings me to the end of my youth days at Mt. Sinai.

Ms. Sonya usually writes the Christmas play. It always teaches a lesson such as how to treat people or having respect for those less fortunate, especially at this time of year. She does a great job involving the youth of the church and sometimes a few adults. She's penned another smash this year.

It's the last night of rehearsal. Everyone's gone except for Ms. Sonya, Link and me. Link's waiting for me to finish so we can hit the mall. I decided to stay after to help Ms. Sonya put away some of the props and set decorations.

"Hey man, give me a hand with this," I say to him.

Link grabs one end of a faux stonewall, I lift the other, and we walk toward the storage room in the rear of the fellowship hall. Ms. Sonya walks behind us with an armful of shirts and scarves for the play.

"Careful boys. I'll get the door," she says.

As we get close to the closet, she slips past us to open the door. We carefully slide the prop inside and lean it against the wall. Ms. Sonya moves to the left of us and reaches up to put the clothes in a blue basket on the shelf.

"Ouch." she yells and clutches her left side with both hands. Shirts and scarves go flying in the air and slowly fall and settle in front of the shelf. We dash over to see what's the matter.

"I'm okay. I-I was-I'm a little sore from working out," she says, wrinkling in pain.

All three of us know something isn't right and that she's not telling the truth.

We play along.

"Are you sure you're okay, Ms. Sonya?" I ask.

"Yes, yes. You boys go ahead. Didn't you say you were going to the mall?"

"Yes, ma'am."

"Well go on. I can finish this."

We ignore her, pick up the clothes, and take care of the last clean up details. Although she doesn't say anything about it, we know she's grateful that we didn't leave. She makes sure the church is secure, and we walk her to her car.

"Thank you. You all are so sweet. Now get out of here and go have some fun."

"Anything for you, Ms. Sonya. You okay to drive?" Link asks.

"Yes. Now go on. I'll see you in a few days."

We both say our goodbyes to Ms. Sonya and head over to Mrs. Potts to meet up with Marshall.

Mrs. Potts doesn't live far. It's about a five-minute walk. Marshall is supposed to meet us there. Maybe Mrs. Potts will have some lemon pound cake or caramel squares. Link's grandmother can burn.

Link and I start jogging toward his grandmother's house, realizing we've kept Marshall waiting about a half hour.

"You think he left us?" I say.

"Man, please. He ain't goin' nowhere. He wants to borrow my Funkadelic tape and my camera. Trust me. He ain't goin' nowhere. He wants that tape real bad."

"What do you think's happenin' with Ms. Sonya?"

"I don't know, but something ain't right. When we was puttin' that stuff away in the closet, that woman was in pain."

"Huh? What do you mean? She said she was sore from workin' out, and you know she works out."

"Naw, man. It wasn't that kinda pain. It was sharp. I saw her face. She could hardly breathe. Before we even got to the closet, she was breathing funny. I wonder if it was her ribs?"

"How did I miss that?"

"You weren't lookin' for it and you couldn't see from where you were. I wasn't either, but I knew something was off with her. I don't know what it is, but it wasn't no workout pain."

"Maybe it was gas. Maybe she was holding it, huh?" I know I'm grasping at straws, but I can't and don't want to think of anything else.

"Yeah, maybe."

Link is silent for a bit, then he says, "You know what Sherlock, after today, I think you might be on to something. There's something definitely going on with Ms. Sonya."

"What are you thinking?"

"I can't put my finger on it, but something's up."

"Well man, I'm glad to hear you say that, cause I feel the same way. Something's happening to her but I can't figure it out."

"There you go. Mason 'I know whodunit' Alexander. I guess you're on the case now, huh?"

"Go on with that. I'm just — "

"You just gettin' ready to jump in feet first."

"No man, I just — "

"It's cool. I'm actually with you on this one. Something's not right. But in the meantime, you to hurry yo' ass up. You run like your sister with a wooden leg."

"Yeah, but at least I don't run as slow as yo' baldheaded mama."

I catch myself quickly, remembering too late that Link's mother is dead.

"Man, I'm sorry. I was just playing. I didn't think about what I was sayin'. My fault."

"It's okay. Don't worry about it. Just don't do it again, or we'll have a problem."

"I thought you said Marshall won't leave us."

"He won't, but let's go."

I hang my head knowing I really did hurt my best friend. What a jerk.

Finally, I break the silence.

"I hope Marshall hasn't left us."

"He won't, but let's hurry up."

CHAPTER ELEVEN

It's two days before Christmas — the night of the program. The fellowship hall is packed — standing room only. Red, white, and green crepe paper and streamers hang from the walls and ceiling. Christmas trees, snowmen, Santa Clauses, and cutouts of characters from the nativity scene also decorate the room. The smell of pine, eggnog, and freshly-baked pound cakes perfumed the hall.

The young children charm the audience — they've got on their freshly pressed suites and pleated dresses, sporting fresh press-and-curl hairdos and recently trimmed cuts. They deliver carefully rehearsed speeches, forget their lines, sing off key, and enjoy themselves. The audience loves every minute.

The play, the capstone of the evening, goes extremely well. It tells the story of a relationship between a homeless girl in middle school and her caring male classmate. The boy learns accidently that the girl is homeless. He's careful not to expose her secret as she asked, but faces challenges in trying to help her. It's a moving play with comedy, drama, and proverbial lessons.

Ms. Sonya has a knack for weaving those kinds of nuggets into her plays. The audience meets the end of our performance with cheers and a standing ovation.

When we take our bows, I see Rhonda standing on the left side of the hall in the middle of one of the rows of gray metal chairs. Our eyes meet briefly, but I have to watch what I'm doing or I'll fall off the stage.

What's she doing here? I wasn't expecting her.

The ovation calms and Rev. Tremmel makes his way to the middle of the stage.

"I want to thank all of you for your continued support of our annual Christmas program. Aren't these children something else?"

The audience responds with applause and shouts accolades to us.

"That's right. Those are our babies."

"I'd like for our visitors to please stand," Rev. Tremmel shouts over the audience.

As people rise, the sound of metal folding chairs with rubber tips rubbing across the floor fills the room,

"All right. What a turn out." Rev. Tremmel continues to yell. "I see we got folks from Pine Hill Chapel in Keerville City." The crowd gives a round of applause. "A group from Holly Grove way out in Hagerson County," and another round. "And we even got some people from Sweet Hill Pentecostal and Bible Way in Claxton. Thank you all so much for coming. Oh I can't forget Rev. Smith, Rev. Rose, and Rev. Alison."

As the applause dies, Rev. Tremmel raises his hands to quiet the audience.

"I have a special visitor tonight. "

He motions to a figure in the front.

"Stand up. I want you all to meet my brother, Mr. Richard Tremmel."

No one has seen this guy before, but he and Rev. Tremmel favor too much for them not to be related. Rev. Tremmel has mentioned in passing that he has siblings, but doesn't' say how many or much about them. He told us that he was the oldest, but not much else.

Richard introduces himself. "Yes, I'm Richard Tremmel. I just arrived from New York to visit my brother and sister-in-law for a little bit."

Of course all eyes from Mt. Sinai examine and probe this special guest. Richard and Rev. Tremmel are nearly the same height. He's considerably darker than Dexter, with light brown eyes and black wavy hair cut short. He wears a neatly trimmed goatee, which frames his straight pearly whites. He looks to be a few years younger than Rev. Tremmel.

Richard is as smooth as his brother.

"You all look so lovely this evening. I was so moved by what Sonya has done with these children. I was so blessed by their voices and speeches. It made me think about how I used to do the same thing when I was their age."

The audience smiles and nods in agreement.

"It's great to be "in the house of the Lord one — more time."

"Say it son," Rev. Tremmel says.

"And I'm looking forward to getting to know everyone."

I'm listening to him, but I'm plotting the best and quickest way to get to Rhonda as soon as they finish.

I'm standing next to Mrs. Carrington, one of the regular members of Mt. Sinai, and she's sitting next to Mrs. Jackson — the same way they sit in church every Sunday. I overhear Mrs. Carrington when she whispers to Mrs. Johnson: "That's a fine looking man, but girl I can tell he ain't nothin' but trouble. But I tell you if I was 20 years younger — Lord have mercy."

I guess a deaconess can get aroused like any other woman.

Mrs. Jackson, gives Richard another once over, nods and smiles big. Other women are cutting their eyes at him, thinking how they can make his acquaintance.

"Thank you Richard for those kind words. I want you all to know that that my brother is an accomplished organist and singer."

Oohs and aahs come from the crowd.

"Starting next Sunday, Richard will serve as our Minister of Music while he's here."

His announcement is met with applause. Since we've never had a Minister of Music before no one seems to have a problem with this — except, my man, Mr. Johnson.

His negative reaction is right on cue. He's sitting near the back on the right. He doesn't say anything out loud, but the sour look on his face and his shaking head say it all. Mrs. Winston is sitting in the row ahead of him. She turns around, and I see Mr. Johnson mouth, "What the hell?" Mrs. Watson shrugs her shoulders and turns her attention back to Rev. Tremmel and Richard. Mr. Johnson's slumped shoulders and dropped head display his acceptance of defeat from this surprise.

"Richard, Give them a sample," Rev. Tremmel says.

From his seat, Richard starts singing the last verse of "O' Holy Night" *a cappella.* If I had my eyes closed, I'd swear Al Green is sitting there. He's moaning, twisting, and squeezing every ounce of feeling out of the melody. Before he gets through two lines, the audience is on their feet going crazy.

"You better sing boy."

"Sing that."

"Lord have mercy. That boy can sang."

When he reaches the last line, "O night divine," he holds the syllable "di." As he's holding the note strong and flawlessly, he stands up, walks on stage, puts his arm around his brother, throws his head back and blows the roof off the building with the second syllable, "vine." and finishes the song.

I look at Mrs. Carrington. She and a few other women look like they might faint.

When Richard finishes, the applause is deafening. People are screaming, fanning themselves, waving their hands, amazed at what they've heard.

A peculiar thought enters my mind from I don't know where — they've been hypnotized. I'm not sure what that means, but I feel like that's what just happened. I bet both of them could do anything they want right now and get away with it. Wow.

The audience wants more. Rev. Tremmel smiles and says, "You got to come back Sunday."

He then summons Ms. Sonya to the stage, as he does every year.

"I want to say publically how much I appreciate what my wife has done with this program. I'm so proud of her and them."

Ms. Sonya waves to the audience.

"Thank you, Rev. Tremmel," she says. "Thanks to all who worked in getting this together. I won't name names because I will forget somebody, but thank you all very much."

She looks up at her husband and smiles.

I'm standing on the floor near the middle of the stage where they are, and although it isn't visible, I can feel awkwardness and tension in her.

I'm looking at Ms. Sonya, scanning her frame in search of bruises, scratches — anything.

He smiles back, takes her hand, leans down and kisses her softly on the cheek. The women are in awe and sigh deeply.

Once Rev. Tremmel finishes and dismisses everyone, I move quickly toward the left section of the hall, carefully wading through the meandering group.

I'm greeted by countless pats on the back and kind words regarding our performance. I'm grateful but can't stop to talk. I'm on a mission.

Rhonda sees me coming towards her and moves out into the aisle. I'm so glad to see her. But now that I'm standing in front of her, I don't know what to do. Hug? Handshake? What do I say?

"Hi. You guys were great." she says.

Good. I don't have to worry about breaking the ice.

"Thanks. It was a lot of work but a lot a fun. I'm glad you came."

"Me too. I must confess that I have another motive for coming. I have something for you."

I'm baffled. We don't have a class assignment due now. She's given me back all the books she's borrowed. What could she have?

She reaches into the medium sized black purse hanging from her shoulder and pulls out a rectangular dark blue box. A red ribbon wraps around the middle, and a bow lay on the top.

"Merry Christmas."

I'm flabbergasted. I manage to say, "Thank you? But I didn't — "

"You weren't supposed to get me anything. Open it."

Dep's standing a few rows away wearing a goofy grin.

I force my opened mouth closed and carefully pull the ribbon from the box.

"Wow, Rhonda. This is so cool."

It's a pen. Not just any pen. It's a beautiful 8-inch golden brown calligraphy — or dip pen with a set of 12 stainless steel nibs. It's absolutely gorgeous.

"Wow," I say, "I've got Esterbrooks and Watermans, but this is a Wasp Addipoint. In the 1940s they started designing these for the military so they would fit in their front shirt pockets."

"What? How'd you know that?"

"Oh," I stammer, embarrassed. "I love pens. I probably know a little more about them than I should."

"No. You just know your stuff. I wanted you to have this. I know how much you like calligraphy and you're really good. I also want you to know how much I appreciate what you've done for me."

"But I — "

"You've done more than you know. And please don't go out and get me anything. I just want you to have this."

My emotions are everywhere, but I'm thankful for this gift. It's special, and even more so because of who gave it.

"Thank you."

I give Rhonda a big hug. As we embrace, she whispers, "I want to finish telling you what I started at the dance before we were interrupted. "

"Okay."

We agree to meet the day after Christmas at Smith's Drugs, the local pharmacy.

CHAPTER TWELVE

Even with all of its enigmas, Christmas is always a great time. But I was one of those inquisitive annoying children who asked too many questions about this Santa Claus guy. The whole thing was perplexing to me. How could a fat white man come in our house, and we don't have a chimney? How can one man and his elves get around the world in one night in a sleigh pulled through the air by eight reindeer? Does he have children? Do they get their stuff first or last?

Yep. Questions like that would get on anybody's nerves after a while, but that was me as a child — always trying to figure out stuff.

Of course the Claus mystery has long since been revealed, but it's still a special time — especially at the Alexander house.

Traditions continue — exchanging gifts with family, the smell of the coniferous tree with the heirloom star on top scraping the living room ceiling. My grandparents have arrived with presents in hand. We smother them with hugs and kisses. Everyone's favorite delectable foods cooking — ham, collards, macaroni and cheese, homemade biscuits, stuffing, gravy, and sweet potato pie. This day puts everyone in a great mood. Phone calls from friends and family near and far. Everything seems right with the world — if only for a little while.

By the early afternoon the guys in our group are making our rounds. We usually go to each other's houses to hang out and see what we got.

The warm spell continues. The gang's now at my house, and we're shooting the breeze in the front yard. Marshall and Mitchell entertain my baby sister by pushing and pulling her in her new red wagon. I think this five-year-old has a crush on Mitchell. She smiles and giggles at all of the attention.

My grandmother gave me an official NFL football, and Link, Dep, and I zip passes back and forth across the yard.

In typical fashion, Link and Dep argue over who can throw the best spiral.

"Look at that wounded duck." Link says about Dep's pass.

"Get outta here. At least mine don't look like a punt."

Cars pass on the road that runs in front of our house. Passengers and drivers wave to us, which is customary in the South, especially on Christmas Day. We know a lot of them. Some even toot their horns.

This is also the first chance we've had to talk about the play and what happened there.

"Hey, man, the play was pretty good," Mitchell says, as he adjusts one of the wheels on my sister's wagon.

"But they need to stop letting them children sing so many songs. They were terrible."

"Man, they just kids," Marshall says.

"So what? After a while that got on my nerves."

"Okay. I hear you," I say. "But let's talk about something else. You gonna give my baby sister a complex."

She isn't paying attention to our conversation. The wagon and the ride she's getting have her engrossed.

"All right then. How about that Richard? That cat can sing, man." Mitchell says.

We all agree.

"I think more people will go to Sinai just to hear him."

"I hate I missed him," Links says. "He's that good?"

"He's *that* good," Mitchell says.

"Anything happen after that? Me and Marshall left right after Richard's song.

"Oh y'all missed the pen. Dep yells.

"The pen?"

"Yeah. Rhonda gave my man a nice pen for his writing stuff."

"My man." Link says, with a big cheese-eating grin on his face.

I downplay the gift.

"She was just thanking me for my work on our project," I say, trying to clarify to them and even myself.

"Okay," Dep says. "That was a nice ass thank you."

"Go on man. It's just a pen."

"Yeah, it's just a pen. But I might look at it as — "

He stops and stares.

"Hey y'all, ain't that Rev. Tremmel? Dep asks. We look to our left and see a black Monte Carlo cresting the hill toward us.

Given what I saw with Ms. Sonya's arm and his eye raping at the mall, I'm not sure what to think of Tremmel anymore. Besides, this cat still hasn't paid me my fifty bucks. That would've made a nice Christmas present.

"Yep, that's him." I say. "It's Tremmel and his brother."

Richard's driving. We all wave as they drive past us. Richard and Tremmel return the gesture, but they're talking intensely and focused on where they're going.

"I wonder where he's headed on Christmas Day? Didn't he say he was going to New York for the holiday?" I ask. Dep remembered hearing that too. The rest of the guys shrug and go back to what they were doing.

Dep continues to watch the car until it disappears.

It looks like Dep lost his train of thought about the pen. Good. Now he has a perplexed look on his face.

"Mason, I seen that guy somewhere before."

"Who?" I ask.

"Tremmel's brother. I know I seen him somewhere before. I just can't remember where."

My sister's trying to pull her wagon with her doll seated against the rear railing but the front wheel hits a crevice in the ground, and the whole thing turns over. She screams in frustration at the top of her lungs. Marshall goes over to help her. The giggles start again.

CHAPTER THIRTEEN

It's almost time to meet Rhonda. I don't know what to expect. I can barely contain myself. I agonize over what to wear. Which shirt? My sisters think I look good in the blue one. Okay, I'll wear it with my dark blue jeans. Okay. Oh no. Are the creases straight? Crap. Is that a spot? Am I too dressed up? Not dressed enough? Should I wear cologne?

I ask my sisters about my final selection.

"What do you think?"

"You look good, Mason," my oldest sister says.

My middle sister says, "You look all right, but you still got a big ol' head."

"Yeah, but you gotta five head instead of a forehead." I say.

"I'ma tell Mama. Mama. Mason in here talking about — what did he say — oh, he said I gotta five head."

"Mason." my mother yells. "Leave that girl alone."

"I'm just playin' with you girl. Ain't nothing wrong with your head."

I give her a gentle tap on her forehead as I walk down the hall.

She swats at me and misses.

"You make me sick." she says, grinning all the while.

I get final approval of my attire from them and make my way to the drugstore. It's not as warm as it has been, but I still don't need more than a light jacket.

Pulling the pharmacy's glass door open causes the bell at the top of the frame to ring. Rhonda is sitting at one of the tables in the back. She looks up when she hears the bell.

I gulp, wipe my sweaty palms on my jeans, and make my way down the aisle toward her. Her smile eases some of my angst.

"Have a seat.' she says. "I wanted to get out of the house, so I got here a little early. I was reading a little Zora Neale Hurston — her short story — 'John Redding Goes to Sea.' "

She points to the book.

"I love the way she writes. The dialect her characters speak takes a little getting used to — but it makes them so real."

"Yeah, I remember trying to read a few of her stories. It was tough, but I think I gave up too soon."

"You should give her another try — and don't give up so easily."

"Maybe I will. I'm glad you got here and got a table." I pause a moment trying to think of something to say. "Do you want anything? My treat."

"Aren't you sweet, Mason. I'll take a Sprite."

"That's all?"

"Yes. I'm not hungry right now."

The teenaged attendant behind the counter fills two white paper cups with crushed ice and soda from the fountain.

"Thanks. So how was your Christmas?" Rhonda asks.

I give a snapshot of the day and ask about hers.

She says it was fine and quickly changes the subject. We small talk about current events, music, and what's happening at school.

"Well enough of that. I'm sure you're wondering why I asked you here, and what I've been trying to say to you since the dance, right?"

I nod. "The thought has crossed my mind a few times."

She smiles and looks around to see who's near. There's no one.

"Well, you need to know that your Rev. Tremmel, and I use that title lightly, isn't what he seems to be."

I'm baffled, but I can't let her know that. What in the world does he have to do with anything? He owes me fifty bucks and there're questions about what's going on with Ms. Sonya. But what does he have to do with Rhonda? Why is she bringing him up?

I control my facial expression and keep it neutral.

"He's been making my mother sleep with him since he got here. He's a bad man, Mason. He even makes my mother do things with other men that she doesn't want to do. He's been doing this for years and nobody knows. Nobody in Grimmel knows this side of him. He's awful."

She picks up momentum.

"What makes matters worse is that his brother Richard is in on this. He's terrible too. Just horrible. I know that you saw him for the first time at the Christmas program, but I've seen him lots of times before. I just couldn't say anything."

I flash back to the Christmas program. Rhonda had tears rolling down her face when Richard brought down the house with his rendition of "O Holy Night." I thought she was just moved by his singing.

I also remember Dep said he's seen Richard before too.

She pauses, looking at the attendant wiping the counter.

"What do you mean? You've seen him before — lots of times?"

"Rev. Tremmel and his brother are — I'll just say it — nasty, stinking, roguish pimps. Tremmel's a murderer too. They're sneaky, conniving, low-lifes. What they do is find girls, women, especially weak ones, and they charm them with their smiles and money.

"Sometimes Tremmel uses his collar like a magnet. He and Richard do whatever they need to do to gain the woman's trust. Then they put them in compromising, precarious sexual situations, take pictures and film them — and blackmail them. They've got women in Maryland, Virginia, North Carolina, and God only knows where else. They do this all the time."

Tremmel? Richard? Ms. Sonya? Ms. Franks? Something doesn't make sense.

But why would Rhonda make up something like this?

"I saw them Christmas morning. They drove past my house."

"Yes, they probably just left my house."

"Excuse me a minute, Mason."

I stand as she leaves the table.

My head's swimming. Breathe Mason.

When Rhonda returns from the restroom, she says something new and startling.

"Nobody knows yet but Ms. Sonya's gone. She left Rev. Tremmel. Finally. Tremmel and his brother have been doing the same things to her that they're doing to my mother."

"What? Are you serious?"

"As a heart attack."

"Why doesn't your mother say something? Why didn't Ms. Sonya say something?"

"They're afraid — and for good reason. It goes much deeper than you can imagine. Tremmel and Richard are blackmailing the heck out of both of them and a bunch of other women. And they don't make false threats.

"Remember last year that story on the news about that really pretty lady that jumped off the bridge and drowned in the Appomattox River in Dinwiddie, Virginia?"

"Yeah. She was an executive for some big company in Atlanta, right? It was strange, because they couldn't figure out why she went to Dinwiddie to do that when she lived in Atlanta. She was like 25, 26 years old?"

"Yes. Let's just say she didn't jump. That was all Tremmel and Richard. My mother told me. She heard them talking about how they did it. They were drunk at my house and bragged about it in front of her. They were blackmailing this woman, and she threatened to tell the police what they were doing to her. So they drove her to Dinwiddie, killed her, and made it look like she committed suicide."

My mind's spinning. The people Rhonda's describing are foreign to me. I sit in disbelief and disgust.

"These people you're talking about sound despicable."

"That's exactly what they are. Years ago when he lived in Maryland, they did the same thing. They did it to my mother and Ms. Sonya. They charmed them and a bunch of other women, drugged them, and Tremmel and his brother took pictures and movies of them doing sexual things with men and women. He did this to Ms. Sonya before they got married. He knew my mother from his college days and manipulated her. They've been threatening them for years about making the pictures and movies public if they don't do what they tell them to do, or if they try to leave or ever say a word.

"He knew your mother from his college days?"

"Yes, they knew each other when they were at Maryland State."

"Whoa."

"Are the movies and pictures that bad?"

"Evidently so. I've seen some of the pictures of other women they're doing this to. If they're anything like those, it's horrible."

"Wow."

"Tremmel told my mother and Ms. Sonya that no one would ever believe either of them over him.

"You've heard the lies about my mother. Tremmel perpetuated those to control her. Yes, she had me out of wedlock, and the questions about who my father is have been settled for a long time, but they won't' let it rest. He was with my mother and they were about to get married when they were living in Maryland. He disappeared just before I was born. The police suspected foul play, but they never solved the case. But that's still not good enough for people.

"My mother's not a whore. She never slept with anyone's husband, but Grimmel folks will believe anything if it's juicy enough."

Ms. Franks' reputation in the community isn't good. I'd heard church ladies tell young wives to keep their husbands away from "that jezebel."

She, like Rhonda, is gorgeous — milk chocolate flawless complexion, thick black shoulder length hair, and a shapely figure. She's so warm and friendly. These features can be a deadly combination with some of the jealous, insecure women in Grimmel. So with just a few words, Tremmel easily exploits the townsfolk's incredulous thoughts about her and now they're nearly indelible.

"Tremmel and Richard come by and — "

She stops. It's like she's seeing the words she wants to say.

"They beat and — "

"It's okay."

"It's just hard saying it out loud. They beat my mother. They make sure they hit her where it doesn't show. And they — rape her. They do it whenever they get ready. They make her do whatever they say."

I'm trying to absorb all of this. Richard and Tremmel?

"Even before his brother made his recent move to Grimmel, when Tremmel would go on his alleged business trips or attend his "conferences," (she makes her quotation marks in the air), he would make my mother go with him. They'd leave in the wee hours of the morning or late at night and meet Richard in another city — in some sleazy hotel. Some of the other women would be there. A bunch of nasty men would be waiting.

I can't imagine this happening.

"Men still pay top dollar to Tremmel and his brother to do vile things to — my mother."

"Although she keeps herself together publically, she drinks sometimes to numb the pain and to escape her reality for a while."

Rhonda pauses and puts her head in her hands for moment. She lifts her eyes and looks to her left, as if she's searching for the right words to say.

"It's driving me crazy, Mason. I just had to tell someone, and you are the only person in this whole town I really trust."

I don't know what to say or think.

I have mixed emotions. I love Ms. Sonya and Tremmel — even though he owes me 50 bucks and he's a ridiculous ogler — but I'm having a hard time wrapping my head around this.

I have to let this marinate.

My intuition told me that something wasn't right between Ms. Sonya and Tremmel — what with the bruises on Ms. Sonya's arm, the possible injury to her ribs, her demeanor. And now this bombshell Rhonda just dropped.

But Tremmel and Richard? Pimps? Abusing Ms. Franks? Ms. Sonya? Right under our noses.

What have they done to Rhonda? If they did something to her, I don't know what I'll do. Rhonda's my friend, but this is a lot to handle.

She continues.

"Tremmel and Richard came by our house Christmas morning looking for Ms. Sonya. It looks like she slipped out of the house in the middle of the night.

"I don't know if you know this, but Ms. Sonya and my mother knew each other from Maryland and are friends. Sometimes when Tremmel and Richard were getting calls from men that wanted more than one woman, or — I hate even thinking about this — wanted to see women sleep with each other, they would take my mom and Ms. Sonya."

"What?" I gasp.

"The morning they came by our house, they were acting crazy, threatening and screaming at us, asking over and over again where Ms. Sonya was."

Damn. I wonder where Ms. Sonya went?

Rhonda reaches in her bag and pulls out a small plastic bottle of lotion. A dab drops from the bottle, and she briskly rubs her hands.

"Want some?"

Maybe she's trying to tell me my hands are ashy.

"Yes. Thank you."

I mimic her. Hmm, this smells pretty and sweet. It smells like Rhonda.

"Mason, you must promise me you will tell no one what I'm telling you now."

I just look at her.

"Promise."

"I promise."

We look into each other's eyes to seal the deal.

"They were right," Rhonda says. "She did come by. Ms. Sonya came by and begged my mother and me to go with her, but my mother was afraid. She was worried they would catch us, so she refused."

"What happened?"

"Ms. Sonya said she was leaving anyway, no matter what and that she couldn't take it anymore. 'I'm sick of the beatings, the deception, smiling for the public. I found negatives and movies in a lock box hidden in the floor of the shed in the back of the house. I haven't had a chance to check who's on them, but I know they'll show girls doing what they did to us.' "

"Did y'all try to stop her?"

"No. She was determined to go. Ms. Sonya told us that it was her only chance and if she got caught, they'd have to kill her.

When Tremmel and his brother got to Ms. Franks' place Christmas morning, they were furious. Rhonda said Richard slammed her mother against the living room wall. He stood over her with clinched fists after she slid to the floor.

"I know she came here. Come clean damn it. What did she say? Where's she going?"

"I told you. I swear. She didn't come here. I haven't seen her. Please leave us alone."

Tears run down Rhonda's face.

"Even though I was scared to death, I yelled at them to leave my mother alone."

Rhonda sobs uncontrollably now. I look around to see if anyone notices, but no one is close. After a few moments, she's composed enough to continue.

" 'Well listen to Ms. Goody Two Shoes," he said to me. 'Shut yo' ass up and sit down. Maybe we'll take you with us.' And then he just turned his back on me, zeroed in on my mother. 'I know you lying woman. But okay. You lucky I ain't got time. But we'll be back though,' " Rhonda says.

Tremmel cornered Rhonda pressed his forehead against hers while he held her hard against the wall and yelled, "Look here you little bitch, y'all better not be lying."

Then he pushed her into the kitchen so hard she slammed up against the refrigerator and slid to the floor.

"When Mama tried to help me, Richard threw her over the living room table, causing her to land hard on the sofa."

"Clean this goddamn place up." he screamed and snatched a biscuit from the stove as he brushed past me and kicked open the backdoor.

"I was so scared that they were going to kill us both."

She assures me that she and Ms. Franks are okay. They're scared because they know Tremmel and his brother will be back. They don't know what will happen then. She and Rhonda don't have any place they can go, at least not right now, but they know Tremmel doesn't make idle threats.

Even though I haven't thought it through or asked anyone, I tell her that she and her mother can come stay with us. She smiles and thanks me, but says they'll be okay.

I sense that Rhonda is drained and our time together is drawing to a close. I glance up at the clock over the magazine section. We've been here for over two hours. It seemed like only minutes. We stand and get ready to leave.

Out of the blue, Rhonda gently takes my hand, looks at me without blinking, and whispers, "Thank you." She throws her arms around my neck and hugs me tight. I feel her breath on my neck and shoulder. I smell strawberries. I hug her back.

We release each other slowly. Her hands slide down my arms and grab my hands. She looks at me once again and kisses me on the lips. I nearly faint. She kisses me again, passionately. I close my eyes and lose myself in the moment. A moment I've dreamed about for a long time. We release each other's lips and maintain our embrace.

Before I could even think or worry anymore about Tremmel, I hear myself asking, "Would you like to go to the movies next Saturday afternoon?"

There's a brief pause. She answers, "Sure."

"Is it okay with you that I don't have a car?"

"Of course. We'll figure out the details later. It'll be fun."

"Sounds good."

I walk Rhonda to the pharmacy parking lot. She's called a cab. Her house isn't far away, but she didn't feel like walking, and her mother was in no shape to drive.

She waves as the cab pulls off. I watch until the car disappears over the horizon. I walk on air all the way home.

Dep and Link stop by later that evening and ask me about my time with Rhonda. As bad as I want to tell them everything, I can't say anything. They can tell something happened, but they assume we made out or something, so they don't pry. They figure I'll tell them sooner or later.

CHAPTER FOURTEEN

It's Saturday. I have a date. I walk to Rhonda's house and we take a cab to the movies. We see *Kramer vs. Kramer*. Great film. After the movie we walk to the only Chinese restaurant in Grimmel for a late lunch and talk about the film. Rhonda is a bit jumpy as we stroll along the sidewalk, looking over her shoulder every few steps. But I squeeze her hand, and she smiles at me.

"It's a shame how the kids get the short end of the stick when it comes to divorce isn't it?" she asks.

"You're right. I don't know much about divorce, but the people I know that have gone through it have some horrible stories to tell."

"Some people shouldn't be parents."

"I agree."

I tread lightly because although Rhonda hasn't experienced divorce, she grew up without a father. I have both of my parents.

"If I get married, it's one time and one time only. I'm not putting my children through that."

"I'm with you." I definitely make a mental note of that.

She says sternly, gritting her teeth, "And if anyone ever puts his hands on me — "

"I understand. You don't have to say anymore."

The date goes as well as the one in my imagination. She's beautiful, engaging, and thoughtful. We continue to get to know each other. It's not too cold, so we walk the streets downtown, holding hands, stealing kisses, window-shopping, fantasizing, and reminiscing about our early school years and youthful experiences.

We laugh and talk, and before we know it, we're back at her house. Because we went to see a matinee, it's still early. I'm aware that we've been together a large part of the day, so I don't want her to get tired of me.

I prepare for good-bye. I take her hands in mine and kiss her lightly on the lips.

"Would you like to come in for a little while?"

I didn't expect that question or invitation.

"Is your mother home?"

"No. She's was tired of just sitting around scared waiting for Tremmel, so she's hanging out with Roxanne, Peggy's mom. They usually get together once a month, and sometimes play cards into the wee hours of the morning. Mom just wanted a normal evening."

"Really? Is it okay? If she comes back early and sees me here, she won't kill me?"

"No. She likes you. Relax."

I step in the front door, and it empties into a beautifully decorated living room.

"Rest your bones Mason."

"Thank you. Your house is beautiful."

"Thanks. We try to make it home," she says as she disappears into the kitchen.

I sink into the beige sofa cushions. She's already turned on the television and comes from the kitchen with a tray of sugar cookies and soda.

Sugar cookies. Yes.

"Did you make these?"

"I sure did, Mr. Alexander." She responds. "I made them yesterday. I just felt like baking."

"I'm glad you did. These are one of my favorites," I say, as I pull another one from the Christmas plate. My removal of the cookies exposes red and green holly leaf decorations on the dish.

"Mrs. Winston makes these too," I add.

Crunch.

I hope she doesn't ask me whose is the best. Rhonda's cookies are good, but Mrs. Winston put her foot in hers. Maybe it's experience. I'm sure Rhonda will get better.

"So, when did you have Mrs. Winston's cookies?"

"I did some work for her the other day, and she had some."

"Hmm. So whose tastes — "

"You know what?" I say on purpose, as I know what she's about to ask, and don't want to open a can of worms.

"When I was over at her house cleaning out her attic a box turned over with a load of pictures. Some of them were old pictures of town folks when they were young. You know, back in their heyday. Some of them were funny. They had — "

"Really? Who did you see? Who did she have pictures of?"

"Well, there was Mrs. Potts, who was really pretty."

She laughs. "Mrs. Potts? I mean not that she's ugly or anything. It's just hard to imagine her — young."

"Yeah, but she was, and she looked good. There were some of Mrs. Winston and Mr. Johnson, and they looked good too. You'd be shocked."

"Really?"

"Yes. The clothes, shoes, shiny black hair. They were something."

"I can see it now," Rhonda says, looking up slightly, as if she can see them. "I really like the styles from back then."

As she talks about her specific fashion likes, it clicks. While I look at Rhonda, I remember more about the pictures. There were pictures of little girls, no more than one or two years old. One of them looked a lot like Rhonda. I wonder if — "

"Don't you Mason?"

My mind rewinds quickly. She's still talking about fashion and hairstyles — I hope.

"Yes."

"Me too."

Thank goodness I gave the right answer.

"Is your grandmother from New York or somewhere up north?" I ask.

"No. She was from here. But she moved to New York eventually. Why do you ask?"

"I saw a picture of some little girls when I was at Mrs. Winston's. One of them looked like you — like your mother. Like a younger version of her."

"Really? Are you sure?"

"Yes."

"You know, it could be. I've heard my mother talk about her mother being friends with Mrs. Potts, Mrs. Winston, and some other people I don't know. But they spent some time in New York in their younger days, so it might have been her."

"That's cool."

I pull out the watch and show her the picture inside.

"Do you think this little baby might be your mother too?"

"Hmm. Hard to tell. The picture isn't that clear. Could be. It could be the boy," she says, as she studies the picture like a trained sleuth.

"Who's the man?" she asks.

"Take a real good look and think, 'Deacon.' "

She does.

"Hmm. I don't think that's my mother. I've seen other pictures of her when she was little, and she didn't look like that. But — is that — Mr. Johnson? Snuff dipping Mr. Johnson?"

I nod.

"Wow. What a difference the years make. He was gorgeous."

"That's what Mrs. Winston said."

"What happened?"

I explain about his wife, the baby, and the other man.

"Well, that would destroy anybody. I'm surprised he hasn't killed somebody."

My sentiments exactly.

"I'm still not sure who the baby is though."

She pauses.

"Mason, where did you get this picture?"

"Uh, I — "

She laughs. You took it from Mrs. Winston, didn't you?"

"Yes — but I'm going to take it back. She was tipsy and I — "

"Tipsy?"

"Yes, she drinks. But I needed to take the picture to show some people who might be able to tell me who these two are. I was thinking of about asking Mr. Johnson. I just wanted to see if someone could tell me about this baby with Johnson."

"I understand. I'm just surprised that you did that, but I do understand. If that's my mother, why would Johnson be holding her?"

"I don't know, but I hope to find out soon."

"It's a little chilly in here. Would you mind helping me make a fire?"

"Glad to."

We place crumpled newspaper, kindling, and dry wood in the lovely stacked-stone fireplace and a warm fire is going in no time.

"That's much better," she says.

She snuggles under my arm and we watch an *I Dream of Jeannie* rerun.

"You know I had a serious crush on Jeannie when I was a little boy. I had all kinds of ideas about what I would do with a genie."

"Like what?"

"Hmm. Well, I'd definitely ask for money. Not too much — just enough for my family to be comfortable. Probably a car. Say a Mercedes. And I'd probably ask to be better looking."

"Really? I can see the other things, but better looking? What do you think is wrong with you?"

"C'mon. Look at the guys at school the girls like. Light-skinned, curly hair, tall. Built. Athletes. That's the standard to being fine."

Rhonda shakes her head.

"Mason, you've got a lot to learn. Some girls are into superficial stuff like that, but a lot aren't. Don't doubt yourself."

She's channeling Link.

Rhonda takes my hand and says, "Come with me." She pulls me off the couch, and we head through the kitchen and out of the backdoor. There's a black 1965 Ford Mustang sitting next to a huge magnolia tree in the backyard. Weeds have grown up some around the tires, but the rest of the area around the car is short.

"Wow. Is this yours?"

"Sort of. It's my mother's. There's something wrong with the transmission or something like that, so it's back here until she gets it fixed. This is where I go to think and get away from things."

"Really?"

"Yes," she answers, as she opens the driver's side door. "Climb in the backseat."

The car is incredibly clean for one that's been sitting in the backyard. She climbs in the backseat with me and closes the door.

"So what do you think?" she asks.

"Man, this is cool." I say. "I'd love to see it on the road."

I look around inside the car. Beautiful black interior. It's immaculate.

"Are you cold?" she asks.

I'm starting to get a little chilly, but I say, "No, I'm all right."

"Well, I am."

She reaches in her pocket and pulls out a key on a little chain from *Dirty Harry's*, puts it in the ignition and turns it forward. The vehicle starts. She turns on the heat, and soon the warmth circulates through the car. She also turns on the radio. The Miles Morgan's Slow Jam show is on WGML.

"How's that?" Rhonda asks.

"Great."

"Oh. I almost forgot I left this in here." She leans up, reaches into the front passenger seat, grabs a big blue blanket, and spreads it over us.

"I like to snuggle up in this when I come out here at night."

Earth, Wind and Fire serenades us with their ballad, "Reasons."

We settle under the blanket, look through the windshield and watch the trees slowly being swallowed up by the darkness. The back porch light on the far end of the house and the glow from the radio illuminate just enough for us to see each other's faces. I'm reminded of our time on the bench at the dance.

Rhonda slides closer to me and lays her head on my shoulder.

"So you like *I Dream of Jeannie*, huh?"

"Yeah. Most teenage boys do." I laugh.

"I know," she says, laughing along with me.

"I have a question for you," Rhonda asks. "If you had one wish from a genie, what would you wish for?"

Great question. I think about her inquiry for a minute. I look at her, smile and say, "My wish already came true."

There's silence. She pulls away. Uh oh. I knew I'd mess up eventually. I can see out of the corner of my eye she's looking at me.

"Mason?"

"Yes?"

"I love you."

I swallow hard. I can't believe what I'm hearing. Rhonda said she loves — me? I play her voice back in my head. Those words sound so sweet.

"I love you too, Rhonda. I think I've been in love with you since the third grade."

She slides closer, and we kiss deeply. My hand slides through her hair, caresses her face. Her hand traces the back of my neck, goes under the blanket slides down the contour of my shoulder and arm and comes to rest on my thigh. My manhood grows quickly, and I'm scared and embarrassed. What is she going to say if she finds out? Oh no. She's going to think I'm disgusting. I can't let that happen. I can't make it go away that fast, so I try to shift my body so that my nature isn't so obvious. Too late. Her left hand brushes against it. She pulls back and looks at me.

"Sorry," I say.

"It's okay Mason. That's supposed to happen right?"

"Well — It's —

Rhonda smiles. She plays with my ear lobe and looks into my eyes.

"Mason, I must confess something. I know that I've shared a lot with you about my mother, Ms. Sonya, and what's happened to them, but I've never done this before."

I must have a bewildered look on my face. She explains more.

"I mean I've kissed guys and messed around a little, but that's it."

I smile and look down at the backseat, tracing its form with my eyes, searching for the right words.

"Well, if it makes you feel any better, neither have I."

My mind excavates an encounter with fast Linda Rae.

Last summer at a house party on Angel Street, I ended up in a closet making out with Linda Rae. Her reputation was on the money — fast. She's a pretty girl — incredible body. Everything a teenage boy wants. Hell, she's got everything most men want. But she was trying to take me places I wasn't ready to go. Linda Rae had more hands than a clock factory. She could've de-flowered me right there in the closet, but I wasn't ready, and Lord knows, it was not something I was ready to do with her.

"Really Mason? You've never — "

"Really. I haven't. I'm sorry. I know guys are supposed to be experienced and all, but —

"It's okay. I'm glad that you haven't, and I'm glad you told me."

She hugs me tight and puts her cheek against mine.

"I want to be with you. I want my first time to be with you."

Okay. Now I can't breathe. Rhonda's saying this to me and —

Two virgins? We hadn't talked about sex very much — and definitely not between us. I've never been this far with a girl in my life. But, we're here now.

We kiss again and the passion grows. Many of our inhibitions are gone, but this backseat isn't the living room. Rhonda starts to lie back on the seat. I have my arm around her guiding her down, and *thunk*. We misjudged where she was and she hit her head on the roller arm for the window.

"Are you okay?" I ask.

"I'm fine," she says, rubbing her head and laughing.

It's okay for me to laugh now, so I join her.

Rhonda slides down a bit so her head won't hit the roller arm. As we kiss, I start to maneuver myself on top of her, and I hear, "Mason, Mason, my hair."

I didn't realize I was accidently pulling her hair while I was trying to move around on the seat.

"Sorry. I'm so sorry.

"It's okay."

We're both cracking up.

Earth, Wind, Fire just finished. Love, Tenderness, and Devotion (LTD) is now singing, "Love Ballad."

Thankfully, there're no super human expectations from either of us. We're just getting lost in each other, trying to figure out what happens next.

I try to help Rhonda remove her sweater. She lifts her hands, and I pull, but it gets stuck. There's Rhonda with her hands in the air and me pulling on the garment like a mad man.

"Hold on." she says laughingly through the sweater. She pulls it down, starts over, decides to pull her arms through the sleeves, and then pull it over her head.

"That's better."

We return to kissing and caressing. She feels my body tightening.

"What are you doing?"

"Trying to take off my — "

My right tennis shoe slams into the door glass when I push it off with my other foot.

We laugh some more.

We're nearly naked. My hand gropes her back trying to find the clasps for her bra.

"It's in the front," she whispers.

"Oops. Sorry."

I've never seen a bra that hooks in the front — but I figure it out quickly.

Our instincts take over. I kiss her neck. We bring our naked bodies together under the blue blanket.

Together we discover love making for the very first time.

Rhonda and I lay in each other's arms on the blanket in the backseat, basking in what happened and what it's done to us.

It's not so late, but I decide that I should go. I've been gone from home all day and want to keep my parents' questions to a minimum. I'd phoned them earlier and told them I would be home a little later than my original time. My dad always dug that I did that, and it usually bought me an extra hour or two.

We turn off the car, grab our clothes, and dash back into the house. I get dressed, and Rhonda wraps herself in a multi-colored afghan from the couch. Something about the mix of the fireplace, the afghan, and the afterglow of sex made her look like a dream. She sips a cup of hot chocolate, as I prepare to leave.

She assures me that she's fine and her mother will be home shortly. I take her word and head toward the door. She kisses me gently.

"Be safe, Mason."

"I will. Talk to you soon."

The door closes behind me. I stand in the night air, inhaling as much as my lungs will let me. The air fills my chest, swirls around my body, making me feel even more alive. Tonight's much cooler than last night, but it doesn't matter. I feel great. I think if I got a running start, I could fly home. I decide to walk instead, replaying every second of my time with Rhonda.

The New Year enters with a whimper. There're celebrations, but it feels anti-climatic. A slight buzz about graduation is starting to build, but it will really get going in a few months.

Rhonda and I are officially a couple, but people aren't sure what to think. We're not hiding anything, but we're not the type of people who hang and slobber all over each other in public. We're private, shy, and my boys respect that. Others want to know intimate details, but the best they can do is guess.

Link and I talk. He's really happy for me. He's the only one that knows the depth of my feelings for Rhonda.

"Look at you, man." he says. "You don't know how to act do you? You smiling all the time."

I try not to smile, but I can't stop it. He's right.

"I couldn't beat that grin off yo' face if I had to. I'm glad for you. Just treat that girl right. You got a good one."

Yes, it's going great, but things are still rough at the Franks' house. Tremmel and Richard still come by and do what they do.

Something inside me is boiling. It's been simmering since my trip to the mall with Tremmel. It's coursing through my veins, engulfing my mind. It's not hate, but it's very close to it. I wish I did hate him. Maybe I could spit the fire inside me and burn him to a crisp. He put his filthy hands on Rhonda, and hit her mother. He's not a man. As much I want to hate Tremmel, there's something that won't let me. But I'm pretty damn close.

I put up a good front when I speak with Tremmel, but I see him for what he is.

Last Sunday after church he said, "Hey, Mason. You still writing? Maybe you can come by my office some time and I'll show you a few things."

Man you ain't got shit to show me. Give me a break.

"Sure, Rev. Tremmel. That would be great."

"Hey, if you don't mind, I'd like to borrow some of your pens. I've got some things I'm working on."

I kick him in the throat and watch him roll around in front of the pulpit holding his neck. Then I kick him in the nuts and watch him make a decision on which body part to grab. I do all of this in my mind, and it feels great.

"Sure, you can borrow them. I'll bring them next time."

Marshall and Mitchell don't say much about Tremmel or his brother. They don't know all of the details, but that's by design. We're all boys, but I know the danger of their ugly tempers and vindictiveness — without thinking through the repercussions. After what happened with those two at Eastern Park, I don't want to take any chances right now.

Everyone in our group has grown fond of Rhonda. She's become one of us. They know how much we like each other, and she hangs with our group sometimes.

She's got four new brothers.

They also know Ms. Franks and have gotten closer to her. If Mitchell or Marshall knew what Tremmel and Richard are doing and have done, I don't trust what they might do. It could be ugly.

They do know that Tremmel and Richard are sneaky, so Marshall and Mitchell avoid them. Dep and Link are more even tempered. Marshall and Mitchell, however, are plotters. They may not know everything, but I can sense that they don't trust Tremmel and Richard at all and could easily be pushed into doing something extreme.

"They caught her, Mason," Rhonda says, as we're leaving the library. "They caught Ms. Sonya."

"Where? How?"

"She tried to sneak back home to get a ring her grandmother left her. Why didn't she just leave it? She almost got away, but she didn't realize Richard was outside. He held her until Tremmel got home."

"How did you find out?"

"Ms. Sonya called my mother. But she said she's leaving again. She's just trying to find the right time. I don't know what they did to her — beat her, torture her — but whatever it was, it didn't break her. She's more determined than ever to break free."

"How's your mother?"

"Scared to death. Ms. Sonya didn't say anything to them about coming to see us, but she knows that since she tried to run they're going to watch her like a hawk."

She's right.

CHAPTER FIFTEEN

It's Wednesday. I'm done with classes at 11 a.m. today. That means I can get to the print shop early and work a couple of hours. Mr. Neal is an easy-going boss and lets me work when I can. He likes the fact that I don't need supervision, and, if I say so myself, I'm good at shooting negatives for brochures and pamphlets, and filling print orders. That makes his life easier and saves him a lot of time. Besides, Mrs. Neal loves me.

"How's my Mason today?" she always asks.

I enjoy working for them too. They're sweet people.

Too bad Mrs. Neal can't bake worth a damn. Those salty sugar cookies (how could she destroy one of my favorites?) and sour lemonade can be tough to choke down.

Marshall picks me up from the print shop and drops me at home a little after 2. I walk through the backdoor and hear my mother on the phone in the kitchen.

"What? Where? What in the world? Okay. Call me when you find out."

"Hey, Mama. What's happening?"

She stares at nothing across the room, trying unsuccessfully to put the phone on the hook.

I take her hand and guide it to the hook for her.

Her eyes are full of water. She looks out the window at the oak tree in the backyard and then at me.

"Mrs. Tremmel, Ms. Sonya's dead," she says, as she wipes her overflowing eyes. "That was Deaconess Betty Lee."

She takes a deep breath and pauses. Her trembling fingers slip while trying to turn the pages of her black phone book.

"I gotta call Mary Lee. Where's her number?" she yells out of frustration and the onset of grief. "I know it's in here."

"What in the — What happened?"

"Said they found her in her car in the Jason River," she says between sobs. "I need to call Mary Lee. Where is her number?

"Looks like she fell asleep at the wheel, ran off the road, through the railing and in the river. Lord, this don't make no sense. Where's Mary Lee's number?"

"Here it is," I say, running my finger across the line in the L-section of her address book.

"Thank you, baby."

This isn't happening. I can't believe this. Ms. Sonya's dead? No way.

I hug my mother. She sobs more, but regains her composure.

"Your father will be home in a little while, so don't call him at work. I'll tell him when he gets home."

I also wait a while, get myself together and call the guys.

Mitchell and Dep have heard already. We meet in my room and tell Link and Marshall when they arrive. We're all in shock. I can't tell them what Rhonda's shared with me, but I know something's not right about this. We spend the rest of the day stunned — grieving and reminiscing about Ms. Sonya, trying to digest what's happened.

"I can't believe she's gone," Dep says. "That lady never hurt a soul."

"I know," said Mitchell. "Don't make no sense."

After the guys leave, I call Rhonda. Just like I thought, she's a mess. Ms. Franks is no better. Rhonda says she's drinking heavily and despondent.

"I knew this would happen," she says, trying to control herself. I hear Ms. Franks sobbing and screaming in the background, "No. No."

"I just know Tremmel and his brother have something to do with this. I don't care what anybody says. I know they're involved."

"I think so too."

After what she's told me they've done and what I've seen, I don't put anything past him and Richard. I've got to find out more.

I do my best to comfort her over the phone and assure her that everything will be okay.

Our house is still, thick, and dark with the news and senselessness of this incredible woman's tragic end.

Morning seems to be grieving for Ms. Sonya when it arrives. It feels so heavy. Getting out of bed is a chore. I will my body to sit up and push myself out of the sheets. I feel like I'm walking through fog. My mind is filled with images of Ms. Sonya, imagining her struggling to breath as water from the Jason River filled her lungs. I try to figure out what happened. I know Rhonda's right about Tremmel and Richard, but how are they connected?

I make my way through classes. It's surreal — almost unbearable. People are talking to me, but I can't hear them. Rhonda's not there, but she told me she wouldn't be.

My father takes an early lunch today and gives me a ride to the print shop. Our ride is deafeningly quiet. Neither of us has much to say. My father knows I'm hurting, but he's not sure what words to choose. When we get to the shop, he breaks his silence.

"Son, I'm so sorry to hear about Ms. Sonya. I know you cared a great deal for her."

"Yes, sir."

"I know it's hard. There ain't nothing I can say that's gon' make the hurt go away. But I want you to think about and remember all the good times you had with her. And I want you to be thankful that you had the pleasure of knowing her. A lot of people will never know that. She'll always be with you."

Wow. I didn't know my father was that deep. His words were perfect and right on time. They still resonate.

"Thanks, Dad. Oh, and thanks for the ride. I'm going to walk home."

"All right, Mason. See you at home."

I watched the bumper of the '72 white Ford station wagon disappear behind the hillcrest.

I hear my name called, as I step in the shop.

"Mason."

It's Mr. Neal.

"I'm so sorry to hear about your friend. How are you?"

"I'm okay."

"It's good to see you. Your friend, I — "

"It's okay. Thank you, Mr. Neal. What do you have for me today?"

"Oh, we have a few orders. They're over on the desk."

I walk over and grab the stack.

"I'll take care of these."

I start the work, but images of Ms. Sonya return. The questions. The ideas, what ifs, whys.

Crash.

Oh no. I can't believe I've knocked over a gallon jug of developer. There's amber glass and liquid everywhere.

"It's okay, Mason," Mr. Neal says. "It happens to all of us."

I go get the broom and remember that I left a negative in the developer. I race to the darkroom, but it's too late — the negative is completely black.

"I'm so sorry Mr. Neal."

I can feel tears welling. What is this? I don't cry. I fight hard, but I can't stop them. I can't believe I'm sobbing.

"Mason," Mr. Neal says, as he puts his arm around me, "You're grieving. You just lost your friend. I want you to go home and rest. I can take care of this. Come back Monday or when you're ready. It's all right."

"Okay. Thank you, Mr. Neal. It's probably best that I go home before I destroy your shop."

"You're a good boy. You do good work. Go, take some time for yourself. We'll see you soon.

Mr. Neal pats me on the shoulder, and Mrs. Neal gives me a tight, love-filled hug and a bag of those nasty sugar cookies.

The fresh air feels so good. It helps to clear my head. I think I'll take the long way home.

I walk past the Shady Grove Cemetery, the Morton's Equestrian Riding School, and Mrs. Ray's Florist. That's right — I'll pass Mrs. Winston's place this way. As I get closer, I see that she's in the yard pruning her bushes — the same ones Link and I pissed on.

If she sees me, she's probably going to try to make me work. Maybe if I — "

"Mason, is that you?"

Shit. She's seen me.

"Yes, ma'am. How are you?" I walk reluctantly toward her.

"Oh, I'm fine for an old lady."

She takes off her gardening gloves and places her shears on the rectangle of bricks that supports one of the two white columns in front of her house. She maneuvers from the bottom to the second step of the porch and takes a seat. I join her.

"Sho is a shame about Mrs. Tremmel," she says.

"Yes, ma'am. It's a shame."

"That poor lady drowning like that. Lord have mercy. I'm sure Rev. Tremmel is a mess."

"Probably. I haven't seen him."

"Mason, thank you again for helping me move my things, and I'm so sorry I fell asleep on you."

More like passed out, I think to myself.

"Child, I was worn out."

"It's okay," I say.

"Mrs. Winston, you know there were some things I saw when were looking at your pictures and stuff that I wanted to ask you about."

"Really? What's that?"

I reach in my pocket and pull out the watch and photos. Her eyes widen as if memories and meaning are filling them.

"I promise didn't steal them. I just borrowed them. I especially wanted to ask you about the watch that night, but you — "

"It's all right, son. It's all right. Lord, I ain't seen this in years," she says, reaching for the watch. I put the pictures on the step next to her.

As I hand her the watch, I ask, "Is the picture inside Mr. Johnson? It looks like him. "And who's the baby he's holding? Can you tell? The picture's pretty faded."

There's silence.

"Mrs. Winston?"

"Yes, that sho' is Johnson. Lookin' just as good as he wanted to."

She stares intensely.

"And the baby?"

"Lord. That's — "

She stops. Her mouth opens a bit.

"I -I don't know who that is. It's hard to tell," she says as she squints and turns the watch. She closes it and puts it in the front pocket of her gardening smock.

"Picture's too faded. No, I'm not sure who that is."

I don't believe her, but what am I going to say?

"You want something to eat, sugar?" she asks, as she pulls herself up from the step.

"No thank you. I need to get home."

"Well it was good to see you. Any word on the funeral?"

"I think it's Sunday."

"Sunday? Okay. Take care of yourself."

"Yes, ma'am. You do the same."

I make my way home. My mind is still filled with visions of Ms. Sonya, but questions regarding the baby in the picture have returned as well.

Why is Mrs. Winston lying? What is she hiding?

CHAPTER SIXTEEN

The funeral is today — a chilly Sunday.
 A Sunday funeral?
 That's never happened at Mt. Sinai, but that's what Tremmel wants.
 The air is heavy. I can hardly breathe. Everything's happening in slow motion.
 My family and I arrive at the church early for the wake.
 I walk ahead of them. I need to see Ms. Sonya now. I need to get this over with, then maybe I'll be okay.
 What's she going to look like? A dead Ms. Sonya? My mind's eye can't see it.
 I go in the sanctuary first, and there she is.
 Ms. Sonya, in a pink dress, lying in a silver gold-trimmed casket. Mountains of flowers surround her and nearly cover the front of the church.
 Unbelievable. She looks peaceful. She looks like she's napping.
 I stand over her, looking down — confused, in pain, trying to understand as best I can what's happening.
 This death thing is new to me. It's unforgiving. So final.
 Ms. Sonya, not now. You can't go. I miss you already. God this hurts. C'mon Ms. Sonya. Wake up. Please wake up. I still need you.
 I feel myself falling apart.

I can't look at her very long. I don't want this to be the lasting image in my mind of her.

The church is getting crowded. I look over my shoulder and peep through the door when the usher opens it. People are lining up outside and huddling together to keep warm while they wait.

Dep and Marshall don't go to funerals. I see Link and his grandmother sitting in the back. Wow, I haven't seen Mrs. Potts at Mt. Sinai in a long time. I don't see Mrs. Winston, but Mr. Johnson is sitting in his usual spot.

Mitchell is sitting with his parents near the back too.

Rhonda is staying at home with her mother.

Hundreds of folks with different motives slowly file by her body. Some are there out of love and respect. Others want to see what Ms. Sonya looks like, and what she's wearing. What a shame. Even in death she can't escape scrutiny and ridicule.

The service begins.

The family processes from the rear of the sanctuary to the front. Tremmel and his brother walk next to each other along with Ms. Sonya's parents.

Ms. Sonya is the spitting image of her mother, Mrs. Allen. She told us her mother remarried after her father died some years ago. Mr. Dale Allen, her mother's husband, is frail but alert. He's older than Mrs. Allen, but he does his best to comfort his wife, as she sobs heavily.

Ms. Sonya didn't have any siblings, but cousins, uncles, and aunts fill the pews.

I watch Tremmel closely. He's crying as expected, and so is his brother.

They're both so full of shit.

Rev. Wilson, a pastor from Maryland, presides over the service. He does a good job of keeping things moving.

Surprisingly, there's not a lot of music — Richard sings a solo. He sounds great, but I wish I could turn off my ears instead of listening to this chirping hypocrite. A lady I don't know, also from Maryland, recites a short poem she wrote for Ms. Sonya.

Many people have lots of accolades and effusive praise for her. I got roped into speaking for the youth department. I keep it together pretty well. But it's tough because of how I feel about Ms. Sonya. To see her lying there, gone well before her time, possibly dying at the hands of some foul men, is very hard.

As they prepare to close the casket, Tremmel stands and walks over to Ms. Sonya's body, leans down and kisses her gently on the forehead. He stumbles as he walks away. The church gasps and sighs. Richard helps him back to his seat.

I don't buy it. I think his trip to the coffin and stumble are rehearsed.

After her burial in the cemetery behind the church, we go to the fellowship hall for the repast.

The energy feels strange. Most of the people who were sobbing and screaming a little while ago seem to act like nothing happened. They're stuffing their faces with cornbread, fried chicken, ham, green beans, mashed potatoes, and assorted cakes and pies. They laugh and talk about any and everything.

I don't understand how they can act like this. Ms. Sonya is dead.

I keep my eyes on Tremmel. Between words spoken to them by family and friends, he and his brother converse heavily. Their exchange is intense.

The family finally leaves, but he and his brother take off in his car instead of riding in the limousine. I find this strange, but maybe they have something to do.

Link comes by the house to check on me. We're still in shock.

Link is my boy, and I just can't keep this secret about Tremmel and his brother any longer. I feel like I'm going to burst.

"Link, I gotta tell you something." I study the grain of the wood in the floor, and before I know it, the putrid story I've been suppressing erupts. I tell him everything.

He's surprised but not shocked.

"I think Tremmel's cool and all, but I've never really trusted that brother. Something about him rubs me the wrong way. Has for awhile."

"Yeah, I know what you mean."

We laugh about our time in Ms. Sonya's classes and clowning the ignorant bullies.

But inevitably our conversation turns serious.

We start to scrutinize about how she died. Something's fishy. Captain Butterfield and the rest of our backwoods inbred police department said there was no foul play, but Ms. Sonya falling asleep at the wheel? Come on. Link and I both say that doesn't add up. Ms. Sonya was too cautious and too smart to do something like that. She wasn't driving from Maryland to Georgia in the middle of the night. She was five miles from home.

"Mason, I can see them wheels turning. I'm with you, man. I think something's funky with Tremmel and his brother, but I don't know if you want to mess with this one. Maybe leave this alone."

I don't say anything. I just look at him.

"What am I sayin'? Link says to himself. "I'm telling mystery boy, the black Sherlock Holmes, to leave this alone? Like that's gonna happen.

"Do yo' thing Black Sherlock. Let me know if you need me."

"Always bruh."

Later that night, Dep calls.

"How you doing?"

"I'm okay. What's happening?"

"Man I got it."

"Got what?"

"I remember where I saw Tremmel's brother before."

"Where?"

"You remember a couple of years ago when I took Tony Richard's paper route for a week?"

"Yeah."

"I had to deliver on his route, and it was over by where Rhonda lives. Man, that's a hard route. The houses are a long ways apart.

"I got started early 'cause I still had to be at school on time. I was out there around 4:45 in the morning. This was in the spring, so it wasn't too cold."

"Dep. C'mon man. Get to the point."

"I am. I am."

I rode past Rhonda's house, and that cat Richard was in her driveway. He had some kind of foreign car — a Datsun, Toyota — something like that. Anyway, his car wouldn't start and he was working on it. He was actin' kinda funny, lookin' around like he didn't want nobody to see him. I don't forget a face. Told you I saw him. It just took me some time to remember."

"Thanks Dep. I appreciate it."

"What's up with that guy?"

"I don't know, but I hope to find out."

The next day, Mitchell and I go to the scene of the accident. Like the police said, there're no skid marks. But if she was asleep at the wheel when she ran off the road, there wouldn't be any.

She hit the corner of the railing just before the Jason River Bridge — she didn't crash through it. She rolled down the embankment into the river. The car wasn't completely submerged, but water filled it up to the back window. Supposedly, her head hit the steering wheel when she hit the corner of the railing, knocking her unconscious. According to the police, she never had a chance.

This doesn't work for me. She hit the corner of the railing with the passenger side of her car. But she just clipped it. It may have pushed her or jerked her head forward, but not enough to knock her out. It doesn't look like she was wearing a seatbelt.

I talk to a few people including Rhonda and her mother and figure out that Tremmel and his brother were the last ones to see her alive.

Ms. Franks said that Tremmel and Richard made one of their unexpected visits the day Ms. Sonya died. They came to Ms. Franks' place at 3 a.m. A passerby found Ms. Sonya's nearly submerged car at 5:12 a.m. The authorities said she died around 2 a.m.

Tremmel told the police that he returned from out of town and found a note from Ms. Sonya saying that she'd gone to see a church member, Mrs. Beulah Jenkins. Mrs. Jenkins lives alone and had supposedly called with an emergency.

Tremmel was scheduled to come back around noon, but said he finished his business late the night before, decided to get a good night's sleep and arrived home about 7:15 a.m. He said he was about two hours or so away in Sharp Point, Georgia. Tremmel said he attended a meeting with associates about building a new recreation center and health clinic in Grimmel. The police said that Tremmel told them that since Ms. Sonya wasn't at home when he got there, and the note said she went to see Mrs. Jenkins, he figured she probably stayed with her. He got the call about Ms. Sonya around 7:45 the next morning.

His alibi looks tight, but I still don't buy it. Aside from what Ms. Franks and Rhonda told me, all of which demolish Tremmel's lies, I have some questions.

If a man comes home and his wife's not there, and hasn't been there all night, wouldn't he start to look for her immediately? If she left a note saying where she was, wouldn't he call her?

Yet, the authorities don't question this and neither does anyone else.

And Richard? He was supposedly with Tremmel, so his alibi is the same as his.

Tremmel announced his trip to the congregation months before, and it was on the calendar in the fellowship hall. Several members claim to have seen him and Richard leave for the trip from the church.

I find it interesting that Mrs. Jenkins didn't remember calling Ms. Sonya. But Mrs. Jenkins is senile. She has good and bad days when it comes to remembering things. Nobody lives with her that could say otherwise about her alleged call to the Tremmel House.

Ms. Franks and Rhonda said that when Tremmel and Richard came by at 3 a.m., they'd been drinking and were hungry. They made Ms. Franks cook them breakfast. While they were eating, Ms. Franks asked if they had found out where Ms. Sonya went.

Richard screamed, "What the hell you asking 'bout her for? Don't you ask me a damn thing about her. As a matter of fact, you don't have to worry about that bitch no more. She gone."

Ms. Franks went on with her cooking and didn't say another word.

Rhonda stayed in her room the whole time but she could hear everything. She said that Tremmel and Richard got what they wanted and left about 4:15 a.m.

I can't prove it yet, but Tremmel is guilty as sin. I think the police — especially that redneck Captain Butterfield — are handling him with kid gloves because he's Rev. Tremmel; or, maybe it's because he's done so much in the community. It could also be they don't want to upset the black folks — because they love their Reverend. I know there're some other folks in on this but, I just can't prove it — yet.

It's sad, but there're folks who would kill for Rev. Tremmel, and they won't believe anything anybody says that goes against what they think about this man.

He has them under his spell.

You know, for him to get away with what he's doing, his connection with Butterfield must go deep.

I remember how fast he traced that tag number when BJ spit at us. He talked to Butterfield. Not just anybody could make things move that fast. Something's funky.

It looks like Ms. Franks is right. Nobody will believe anything other than the story Tremmel's giving them.

Tremmel has worked this out. He's discredited and blackmailed the only person I know who can speak against him — Ms. Franks. He even brought in a senile old woman whose memory can't be trusted to take the focus away from him. No one thinks to call the "associates" he was meeting with. I'm willing to bet there aren't any or he has people who will say whatever he wants. And if I'm right, he's even got the police on his side. He made sure people knew his travel plans and saw him leave. He's created the persona and image he wants people to see and believe. It looks like he's gotten away with getting rid of his wife. It looks he's gotten away with murder.

I have to give it to the bastard. He's smart as hell.

But there's no perfect murder. There has to be a chink in his armor somewhere.

I just gotta find it.

CHAPTER SEVENTEEN

It's Saturday, a few weeks after Ms. Sonya's funeral.

I'm supposed to meet with Tremmel at the church at 2 o'clock to talk about Maryland State.

"Mason, pick up two onions and a few carrots on your way back," my mother says.

"Yes, ma'am."

Typical for me, I leave a little early and arrive at the church before two. I walk because it's an incredible day.

I make my way through the sanctuary to his study. As I raise my hand to knock, I hear two voices.

My knocking hand freezes in mid-air.

I recognize Tremmel's voice but not the other.

"Damn, I'm glad we finally got rid of that bitch." The other voice says.

Who are they talking about? Bitch? I know he had problems with his secretary Mrs. Myrtle. He said he let her go because she couldn't keep up. But why is he calling her a bitch?

I get closer to the door so I can hear.

"Yep, It was close."

That's Richard's voice. I listen closely.

"I hated to see her go. She brought in some good money, but she was about to blow everything. I'm glad we're in the South and dealing with these dumbass cracker cops. Butterfield is as stupid and backwards as they come. I bet you his mother is his sister. We got that fool eatin' outta the palm of our hands."

"You right about that." Tremmel says.

I hear glasses tinkling with ice and liquid pouring.

Tremmel continues. "Toss these dumbass honky cops a few dollars and some pussy — you know Butterfield likes that good black stuff — and you can do anything you want. Damn they stupid."

Okay. They're not talking about Mrs. Myrtle.

"You know that's good though, bruh'. Ain't no way in hell they'd ever figure that you smothered her ass and pushed the car off the bridge."

"Yeah, it worked well. Your idea about slamming her face into the steering wheel was a stroke of genius. The crash and water took care of the rest — especially the films and negatives."

Richard says, "What can I say?"

"How in the hell did she find that stuff?"

"She must have been following me, watchin' me. I had them in a box under the floor in that shed behind the house. She had to be watching me. She had no reason to go in the shed. She didn't do shit in the yard. Well, hell, I don't either, but she didn't have no business in the shed at all. That heifer got a good number of 'em, but she didn't get them all."

"Where are the others?"

I hear a lock click.

"I have them locked here in the bottom drawer. I'm taking them with me when I go to Tampa next week. I'll secure a spot there for them. I'll give you the address and a key. I don't know who Sonya might of told."

"You know we're gonna have to do something with Franks and her daughter pretty soon. I can see that heifer's 'bout to break, and her daughter will probably follow suit.

"Yeah, it's about time She's getting' old anyway. It's about time to break her daughter in. She's been marinating just long enough."

"That's some Grade A Beef right there."

I remember Tremmel's reckless eyeballing and search for "Grade A Beef" at the mall.

"Should bring us some long green for a while."

"Oh shit, Richard. That boy Mason will be here any minute. Nice kid, but he worries the hell outta me sometimes."

I hear moving furniture, glasses, liquid pouring, closing drawers and shuffling papers.

"Go out the side door and I'll catch you later at the house."

I nearly break my neck running through the sanctuary jumping over pews and out the front door of the church. Did these fools just say what I think they said? I can't believe what I just heard.

I run home as fast as I can. I make it to our porch, my hands on my knees, panting. I gather my breath.

Okay. Think. What do I do?

I call Tremmel and postpone our meeting.

"Is everything okay?" he asks.

"Yes." I say. "I just had a few things come up that I have to take care of. Can we set up something later?"

"Sure. Just let me know when."

"Thanks."

As I hang up the phone, my mind and heart are racing a thousand miles an hour.

What am I going to do with this? It's exactly what I suspected, but much worse. I don't have concrete proof — but now I know that they did it.

I sit in on my bed and collapse backwards. I outline the ceiling, as I ponder my next move.

"Mason?"

"Yes, ma'am."

"Where's my onions and carrots?"

"Uh — "

"Uh, my foot. Go get my onions and carrots."

"Yes, ma'am.

My feet are on autopilot, as I walk to the market. I keep replaying Tremmel and Richard's words. These guys are murderers, I can't prove it — yet. Murderers in Grimmel. Man.

Okay. I'm supposed to get peas and carrots? Onions and beans? Onions and carrots. Got it. I'll get two of — "

"Mason, is that you?"

Oh hell. It's Mrs. Winston — again. I can't stay away from this woman.

"Yes, ma'am, it's me."

She can see it's me. Why does she ask a question like that?

"You shopping for your mama? How sweet."

"Yes, ma'am."

"You know it was meant for me to run into you today. I need some help with my groceries. My rolling basket done broke, and I didn't drive my car. Can you help me?"

"Well, Mrs. Winston, my mama needs — "

"Why thank you. You such a nice boy. Here, you take these two, I'll take this one. You know I don't live far."

My mother is going to kill me, but if I don't help Mrs. Winston, she'll kill me too.

We walk towards her house, and she won't stop talking. I haven't said a word. I nod every now and then, but her mouth won't close. I hear about her flowers, the neighbor's dog, her bursitis and corns, and what color she wants to paint her house.

We finally reach her porch.

"Thank you, Mason, but wait just one minute."

"Mrs. Winston, you don't need to — "

She shushes me and goes inside.

I should just take off but that would just make matters worse. She comes back outside, takes my hand, and places something in it.

"Here. I want you to have this, and I apologize for lying to you earlier."

I'm lost and baffled.

"What is — "

It's the pocket watch.

"Mason, I should have told you this a long time ago, but I didn't think you were ready. But you are now. The watch belongs to Mr. Johnson. He asked me to hold on to it for him a long time ago. Said he couldn't bear to look at it. You know that's him in the picture. You asked me who the baby was he's holding. I told you I didn't know, and I was lying. The baby is Johnson's son — Dexter Tremmel."

"Rev. Tremmel? Mt. Sinai?"

"Yes," she says. "Mr. Johnson is his father. When he was in the army, Johnson married Lois. Matter of fact, all of us folks from Grimmel was all married — me, Potts, and Johnson. I told you this before. Johnson was crazy about that woman. She was pretty. Light-skinned, long dark brown hair, dimples, cute figure. But she was loose. That hot tail woman flirted with men all the time."

"Mr. Johnson didn't — "

"Child, that man was in love and deep denial. Well, she got pregnant right after she and Johnson got married, and had Dexter. The marriage didn't last. Lois ran off with some man and had Richard a few years later. Johnson looked for his son and found him eventually. Lois was mean, but she let him see Dexter sometimes. That's how he got that picture in the pocket watch. But she disappeared again."

"What happened to Lois?"

"Like I said before, somebody killed her and that man she was with. He thought he was a gangster, and owed the wrong person money."

"This is incredible."

"Johnson kept looking for Dexter. He would see him every now and then. That boy got passed through the system and a few relatives' homes on his mother's side. Johnson found Dexter again while he was at Maryland State. Johnson tried hard to form a relationship with him, but it went bad. Dexter was a slick lil' rascal and used him."

"What do you mean?"

"He played Johnson for a fool. Made him think they were reconciling, but he was setting him up."

"Mr. Johnson couldn't see what Dexter — I mean Tremmel was doing?"

"No. He wanted that boy to love him or at least like him again, so he didn't want to see."

"I understand. So what did he do?"

Mrs. Winston shook her head in disgust.

"That boy drugged Johnson." She pauses and looks down at the cracks in the sidewalk.

"Took pictures and made films of him. Made him look like he liked little boys."

"He did wha — "

"You heard me right."

"So what did Mr. Johnson do?"

"Nothing. What could he do? Dexter threatened him. Told him he better do whatever he say do, or he would show them pictures to everybody."

"But couldn't he have — "

"He couldn't do nothing. Dexter even threatened to kill Johnson if he said anything. The man was scared. Scared of his own son."

"And that's why Mr. Johnson is a recluse?"

"For the most part. He feels it's best if he stays to hisself. Less chance of him getting' hurt or getting' somebody else hurt."

"This guy is something else," I say, shaking my head in disbelief.

"Yes Lord, he sure is. A few years ago, Tremmel called Johnson and said he was coming to Grimmel to take over Mt Sinai. He reminded Johnson of what he said he would do if Johnson opened his mouth. That man don't make idle threats either.

"Lois told Tremmel about me and Flora Potts and our connection to Johnson, and sent word that he would kill us if we uttered a word. He even threatened to kill Link."

"What?"

"Yes. Be careful Mason. Dexter is dangerous. I'm sure there's more that I don't know, but I've kept it all in long enough. It was time to tell you. I felt since Ms. Sonya's passing you would want to know."

"Thank you, Mrs. Winston. Thank you so much. Do you need me to carry — "

"No. You've done plenty. I can take it from here. Go on. Yo' mama is waitin' for you."

I grab the bag of onions and carrots and sprint home. My head's throbbing and bulging, my stomach's churning.

"Here are the onions and carrots." I say, as the backdoor slams shut.

"Boy, what took you so long?" my mother yells.

"I ran into Mrs. Winston, and — "

"Say no more. Go tell your sister to come and cut these onions and carrots for the salad."

CHAPTER EIGHTEEN

It's early May. It's getting warm, but the temperature is up and down.

Tremmel carries on church services as usual. He and his brother work their magic on the congregation. They're a dynamic duo, but I can now see right through their illusions.

The impromptu Christmas performance Richard the murderer gave was a drop in the bucket compared to the show he puts on every Sunday. It sounds like he has four hands when he plays our Hammond B3. Even though I hate myself for it, I'm mesmerized at the dexterity in his feet, as they sweep the pedals. Man, he can make that organ groove. The vibe is so strong. I can sense that people want to dance because what he's playing is so funky. If they only knew they were enjoying the work of the devil's henchman.

Tremmel, the other murderer, continues to give rousing sermons. He's truly full of shit. I'm only there because I have to be. My body is present, but I'm someplace else. I fight to keep anything he says from entering my mind. They're like poison darts that I don't want to touch me. And I've been avoiding him like the chopped spinach.

Since he and Richard killed Ms. Sonya, he's laying it on thicker than usual with the Jesus stuff, and people are eating it up. Folks are shouting and dancing all over the place. It's strange because there wasn't much of that before at Mt. Sinai. Now it's commonplace. Almost expected. I think the way Richard plays has a lot to do with that. If folks only knew who was feeding them.

Each week is standing room only, and they don't disappoint. They put on an excellent show.

It feels like they're trying to make people forget Ms. Sonya.

I can't. I never will.

Every time I see Tremmel and Richard, I see her and what these conniving bastards did.

***

I spend most of the day journaling about Tremmel, Ms. Sonya, what's happening, and what I've learned about her death. It's hard to express my thoughts verbally, so I write about them. I've got to release some of this pressure and scrub my brain.

I hear someone in the kitchen. It's Link.

"Hey, Mrs. Alexander."

"Hello, son," my mother says to him. "How's your grandma?"

"Good. Tryin' to keep me in line."

"You don't give her no trouble, do you?"

"No ma'am. Well, I try not to. Is Mason —"

"Yes, he's back there in his room writing or reading something. You can go on back."

"Thank you."

"Tell your grandma I said, 'Hi.'"

"I will."

I've decided to tell my boys what I heard Tremmel and Richard say, but I want to talk to Link first.

Link comes in my room, just as I finish the last sentence of my journal entry.

"What you writing, man?" he asks.

"Just messin' around. You gonna hang out for a minute?"

"Yeah. Why?"

"I need to tell you something — it's under the pact, okay?"

"Okay."

Under the pact means you can never ever under any circumstances say anything to anyone outside of our group. It's one of the things that binds us like brothers.

"Hold on a sec," I say.

I check to see if anybody's near my door. My sisters are outside. My father's at work. My mother's still in the kitchen.

"Check this out — "

I tell Link everything I heard.

"Whoa. Are you serious?"

"Shh. Keep your voice down."

"My fault. You've got to be kidding."

"I wish I was."

"Are you sure, Mason?"

"Without a doubt."

"Man, I knew you'd find out something if you kept pokin' around mystery boy. You and them damn mystery books."

He walks over to my desk, picks up a book, and thumbs through it. I can tell he's thinking hard.

"I knew those Tremmel cats were funky, but this is deep. Kill your wife? Kill somebody like Ms. Sonya? Damn. They cold."

He puts the book down and looks at me intensely.

"This is definitely under the pact."

The rest of the guys come over. I can tell by the looks on their faces they know something's up.

Marshall and Mitchell sit on opposite ends of my bed. Dep plops down on my red beanbag chair. Link looks out the window at my sisters jumping rope.

"Hey, guys, I got to tell you something. It's under the pact."

Everybody straightens up and listens closely.

I tell them everything.

Link continues to peer out of the window while everyone else looks at the floor. It's as if they are absorbing what I just hit them with.

Funny, none of them are too surprised. They ask the same questions Link did. All including Link want to do something to Tremmel and Richard now.

"We've got to be cool," I say. "We need to see how things play out."

***

School's ending soon.

My fear of speaking to Rhonda Franks has blossomed into something better than I could have ever imagined. I'm linked to this beautiful young lady, and she really cares for me. In the midst of all that's happened this year, I will forever cherish what's developed between us.

We've completed our project and it's stellar work. Ms. Lockhart loved what we did.

"I really enjoyed reading your thesis," she tells Rhonda and me.

"Such thorough work. You make me feel my teaching is worthwhile. I'm going to miss both of you so much, but I know you'll be successful in whatever you decide to do."

"Thank you, Ms. Lockhart." we both say.

She hugs us. We're all a little misty.

It hits me that my time is up with this incredible teacher.

Ms. Lockhart will never know that she was the catalyst in making one of my dreams come true.

Although we're officially dating, we agree not to spend too much time at her house because of Tremmel and Richard. They've been quiet lately, probably trying to lay low until the absence and memory of Ms. Sonya fades. Then they'll probably be right back over their hounding Rhonda and her mom.

***

Ms. Sonya's death won't leave me alone. Even though I know Tremmel and Richard killed her, I need evidence other than what I heard through a closed door to prove it. I continue to search and ask questions. I've just got to figure this out.

I talk to Ms. Franks again. She doesn't tell me anything new, but she says, "You should talk to Mrs. Potts."

I call her.

"Yes, Mason, I'm happy to talk to you. Come by Sunday afternoon around two."

Mrs. Potts is a gracious host. She's a sweetheart. The quintessential picture of a grandmother. Silver hair pulled back in a bun. Large frame glasses. Today she wears a dark green short-sleeved dress with purple flowers.

She opens the door to the screened porch.

"Come on in here boy and give me some sugah. Sho' is good to see you. Boy if you don't look like yo' mama spit you out. Built and stand like yo' daddy though.

"How's yo' family?"

"Everybody's doing fine."

"Good. Please tell them I said, Hi."

"Yes, ma'am."

"Have a seat."

I sit in a large white wicker chair next to a sprawling rubber tree plant. The screened porch is lovely. Flowers strategically place to get sunlight. Everything is so neat. A gentle breeze makes the temperature just perfect.

"Excuse me a second honey," she says.

"Can I help you?"

"No son, but thank you. You stay right there and make yourself comfortable."

There's a picture of Link when he was about five sitting with Mr. and Mrs. Potts.

Glad he grew into those ears.

Mrs. Potts returns with sweet tea and caramel squares for us. Her caramel squares are legendary. I don't want to talk now. I wonder if she'll let me sit here and eat all of those squares?

"Baby, I'm so glad you came by. Mrs. Winston done told me she been talking to you. I've wanted to talk to you for a while. Ms. Franks did good to send you."

"Yes, ma'am."

"Good. There're some things you need to know, and I think you're ready to hear and understand them now."

"You notice that I don't attend Mt. Sinai very often."

"Yes, ma'am."

I look down and see that she's wearing new blue house shoes. She slides them off and stretches her toes through her beige knee high stockings.

"I haven't been too many times since Rev. Tremmel came. People don't know that I knew him before. I tried to tell some of the members about him, but they wouldn't listen. He had their noses wide open. You would think the man walks on water or somethin'. Lord, people are so gullible. It's a shame."

"Baby, hand me that picture over there by that tiger lily."

I stand up and walk toward the plant I think she's talking about, because I have no idea what a tiger lily is.

"That's right," she says.

Good guess on my part.

"Give me that one to your right."

What the — ? It's the same picture Mrs. Winston had of Mr. Johnson and Tremmel as a baby.

I ask, "Is this — "

"Yes, Mason. You saw this when you were at Emma's house. It's Rev. Tremmel — Dexter — as a baby. Yes, he's Cleotis Johnson's son."

I shake my head.

"I know it's a lot to take in. We were all in New York together for a spell, having a ball. Cleotis was finishing up his time in the army, and me and Emma had just gotten married. We was somethin' else. Them folks in New York didn't know what to do with two of the finest sisters from Grimmel. We was married, but we sho' nuff made some wives and girlfriends jealous.

"I believe it."

"Yes, we was fine, married and in love." She looked straight ahead, as if she was watching a movie of what she was describing.

"I'm sorry baby. I'm rambling."

"No ma'am. Not at all." I wanted to hear more.

"Those were some good times." She looked to her left and then back at me.

"Poor Cleotis. He was so pitiful. It was like somebody put a root on him when it came to Lois. He was obsessed with that woman. But she treated him so bad. Talked to him any kinda way. Even after she had the baby, she ran around on him. He was pitiful."

"He didn't try to get her to act right?"

"Child, please. She did what she wanted. I think Lois loved him in some twisted way, but she sho' didn't respect him. Just walked all over him. She finally left with one of them hooligans she ran around with and took the baby."

"Didn't Mr. Johnson try to get control of his son?"

"Some, but it didn't do no good. As the mama, she had all the power. She let Cleotis see him sometime. That's how he made that picture. But that was about it. Johnson paid a little money to her — Damn fool. I wouldn't a paid her a dime. Last thing I heard was she had a baby by the fool she ran off with."

"That's what Mrs. Winston said."

"That must have been Richard," Mrs. Potts says.

"Yes. She also said both were killed — shot by somebody," I say.

"Shame. But it don't surprise me. That woman's mouth used to get her in some stuff."

"So you knew Tremmel was Mr. Johnson's son?"

"Yes, I knew, Emma knew, and I think Carolyn Franks, and of course, Ms. Sonya. But Tremmel threatened all of us, and Cleotis begged us not to say anything. He didn't want no trouble, but we knew he didn't want Tremmel here. Neither did we, but we did what he asked."

"Have you talked to Mr. Johnson about Tremmel since he's been here?"

"No. And honestly, I don't think he wants to talk about how bad he is. That's his only child, and he does all these nasty things. Johnson probably thinks if he had been more active in Rev. Tremmel's life he may have turned out better. I think he's just pure evil."

"Does Tremmel remember you and Mrs — "

"I don't think he remembers none of us. I think his mama might have talked about us when he was little and said something about us living here."

"Has he said anything to you about his mama?" I ask.

"No, has he said anything to you?"

"No, ma'am."

"Other than 'Good morning' and Good evening, he ain't said more than ten words to me. See, he was a little fellow when we were in New York, and we look different than how we looked then. I don't think he remembers us at all, like I said. I don't know what Lois told him. Knowing her, she might have gotten my name wrong — if she remembered it at all."

"When was the last time you saw Tremmel before he came to Grimmel?

"I met him again while he was at Maryland State. He didn't remember me then. At least he didn't act like it. My niece was a student while Ms. Franks was there. Did you know Ms. Franks went to Maryland State University?

"No, ma'am." Rhonda said she was in Maryland years ago, but she didn't say she went to Maryland State."

"Well, she did. She was a very good student too. Smart.

Mrs. Potts pauses and sips her tea.

"She used to date Rev. Tremmel. Well, he was just Dexter then. Didn't last too long. They stopped seeing each other after about a year. Then she met Rhonda's father — Braxton.

"Braxton was a good young man. He loved her and treated her good. But while she was with Dexter, she made a bad mistake.

"See, Dexter got her all liquored and drugged up and made some pictures and movies with her doing sex stuff with a bunch of men and ladies.

"When she started going with Braxton, Dexter got jealous and started blackmailing her — taking her money, making her do unnecessary errands, his school work — but Carolyn got tired of it, and she really liked Braxton. So she broke down and told him what happened. He understood. He told her it was all right and not to worry.

"Well, Braxton confronted Dexter. They got to fightin' in her apartment, and Dexter stabbed Braxton in the chest with a knife he had on him. Killed him. He threatened Carolyn — Ms. Franks — that if she told anybody, he would make sure that everyone saw those pictures.

Dexter made it look like Braxton disappeared and hightailed it outta Maryland."

I'm sure my eyes are as big as saucers. Mrs. Potts is hitting me with some heavy stuff.

"You want another square, baby?"

She knows I do.

"Help yourself."

And I do.

Mrs. Potts goes on.

"Carolyn found out she was pregnant with Rhonda right after Dexter killed Braxton. When she came home to Georgia, she was pregnant with no father of her baby and had to keep her mouth shut about what happened to him. That was the seed for her "reputation" here in Grimmel. When Tremmel came, and I know one of the reasons was to follow Carolyn so he could keep her in check and fan the flames."

"That explains a lot, Mrs. Potts."

"I'm sure it does. Now there's something else I need to tell you. Link loves all of y'all boys. Y'all are the brothers he never had."

"We feel the same way about him."

"I know you do. But Mason, he thinks the world of you and Dep. Lord knows he and Dep argue and compete all the time, but he would do anything for him. Them two boys are so much alike. It don't make no sense. One dark-skinned. One light-skinned. And the way people try to pit them against each other cause they look different. But them boys is two peas in a pod. That's why they act that way toward each other."

She refills my glass and passes me another square.

"He respects and admires you, Mason. He knows that you have a good heart and always try to do what's right. He trusts you.

There's one more thing I want you to know. This is hard." Mrs. Potts pauses and looks over her glasses directly at me.

"Rev. Tremmel killed Link's father."

"What? Are you kidding — How? When? No."

"Yes. His father's name was Daniel Lane. Daniel was a little strange, but real smart. Everyone thinks he went over there to Europe and died in a hiking accident. That ain't true.

"While Carolyn was at Maryland State, Daniel, who was from New York, was there at the same time working on his degree. He didn't have much money, so he worked two jobs to pay for his schooling. He taught piano lessons and worked at a deli near the school. He was here a few times because he was dating my daughter, Lisa, Link's mother."

Link told me his mom's name was Lisa. She was living and working in New York when she got pregnant with him. She died giving birth. She was in New York most of the time she was pregnant with him.

"Mason, wretch around that big yellow vase there and hand me that picture."

"Here you go."

"Take a look at it."

The lady in the frame smiling at me is drop-dead gorgeous.

"That's my Lisa," she says.

I look closer at the picture. She does look like a young Mrs. Potts.

"That girl was so sweet. Wanted to be a lawyer. Smart as she wanted to be. I still miss her."

"What happened?"

"Daniel looked out for Carolyn while she was in school. She told him what Dexter was doing to her, and Daniel threatened him. So Dexter got some of his goons and they jumped Daniel. Beat him to death."

Just like I thought. Mafia don.

"You know, Lisa knew what Dexter was doing to Carolyn, but she couldn't say nothing because she was pregnant. Daniel told her not to worry about it. Said he would take care of it. But I could tell it was tearing her up. She and Carolyn was close, but when she got with Dexter, he kept them apart. I can't prove it, but I swear the stress of knowing what Dexter did to Carolyn helped take the life out of her."

I can barely breathe.

"Dexter cut off Daniel's ring finger with his high school class ring on it and gave it to Carolyn. He told her if she told anybody or did anything else, this is what they will get, and he would show them pictures."

"This man is sick."

"Yes, he is. I know this is a lot for you, Mason, but I wanted you to know. I don't know how much time I have left, so I wanted someone to know just how evil Dexter Tremmel is. I felt that you were the person to tell this to."

"Thank you, Mrs. Potts. It means a lot to me that you would trust me with this." I reach out and grasp her hand.

If only I knew what to do with it.

"I wish my husband was here to see Link all growed up."

"I'm sure he would be proud."

"Yes. Me and Mr. Potts love that ol' boy. He's as sweet as he can be."

She pauses and sips her tea.

As she sips and takes a bite from a square, I look around the screen porch. I notice a pair of men's shoes. The brown backs of them are peeking from under a tan wicker loveseat. I've never seen Link in those. Actually, he wouldn't wear shoes like that. They're too old-fashioned. They look a little big for him too, but they look familiar. Hmm. Mr. Potts has been dead for a long time, so who's are — .

"I see you looking at those shoes."

Uh oh. Think fast, Mason.

"Well, I was just looking — "

"It's all right. I meant to put those things away. Some folks is so nosey."

"Yes, ma'am," I say, hoping she changes the subject. I think I want to know who belongs to the shoes, but then again maybe I don't.

"Well, I've told you this much so far. You might as well know the rest."

"Ma'am?"

"Those are Mr. Johnson's shoes."

"Mr. Johnson?"

"Yes, Mr. Johnson. He and I — keep company sometimes."

"Keep company?"

She smiles slyly at me and raises her eyebrows.

"Oh." I say, finally getting the message. I feel my face turn red from embarrassment.

She laughs. "Mason, it's all right. We grown folks, and we do what grown folks do."

"Yes, ma'am." *Please don't share any details. I don't need to add to the visual I'm already having.*

"You might even see a pair of his shoes under one of Mrs. Winston's chairs too."

The look on my face must convey my emotions. Now I know where he was going.

"It's all right, son. I know it's a lot for you to handle, and I'm sure you will see us a little differently now."

That's an understatement.

"We're just three lonely people finding comfort in each other. We know what we're doing. Been doing it for a long time. Started about a few years after Mr. Potts and Mr. Winston passed."

"I-uh-does Link know?"

"Sure, but just like you, he ain't never gonna tell nobody."

"Yes, ma'am."

"You okay, son?"

"Yes," I say, as I bring the sweet tea to my lips.

"There's something I want you to do, Mason."

"Yes, ma'am?"

"Watch out for Link. Please, always watch out for him. Always. Will you do that for me?"

"Yes, ma'am. I will."

"You know, you should visit Cleotis Johnson. I know y'all don't like him, but just talk to him. He's all right. He might have some history to give you too."

Well, I don't know how much more I can handle. I'm sure he will have a lot to say about Tremmel. But he won't have tea and cake.

"Thank you again, Mrs. Potts."

I wipe my mouth, give her a big hug, grab some more caramel squares and make my way to Mr. Johnson's house down the street.

My head is twisting with all of what Mrs. Potts dropped on me. Mrs. Potts, Mrs. Winston, and Mr. Johnson? My body shivers in disgust and astonishment.

Looks like Mr. Johnson's expecting me. Mrs. Potts must have called him. His front door's cracked. I knock lightly.

"Hello? Anybody home?"

"It's open," he yells.

I enter, stepping over piles of old newspapers and stacks of mail. Mr. Johnson comes out of the kitchen holding an old wire flyswatter in one hand and a tin can in the other.

"Hello Mr. Johnson."

"Hey. Hey." he says. He motions with his head for me to come in. I proceed cautiously.

His house is so hot. And it smells like boiled chicken. Mr. Johnson wears a dingy white tank top t-shirt, old gray dress slacks and black slippers. The ashy heels of his feet hang off the backs. The tin can in his right hand is full of snuff spit, generated by that lump in his lower lip. His heels combined with the boiled chicken smell and that half full snuff cup nearly turns my stomach.

What do Mrs. Potts and Mrs. Winston see?

"Come on in here boy. I know y'all children don't like me, but it's all right. I was a teenager too, ya know."

"Thanks for talking to me Mr. Johnson."

"Yeah, yeah, sit down."

I'm scared to breathe or put my ass on anything in here. I find a space on the edge of an old red faded kitchen chair filled with rags.

"Yeah, me and Potts tried to warn them folks about Tremmel."

He looks at me and makes a deposit in his can. As he wipes his mouth with the back of his hand, he stares out of the dirty window.

"Winston said she told you about my relationship to Tremmel."

"Yes, sir."

"Damn. He wasn't always like this. He was a good boy. Such a good little baby. Used to call him Moonbeam. His mama — "

Mr. Johnson stops and goes to a desk in the far corner of the room. It's hiding under mounds of papers and boxes. He opens the bottom right drawer and pulls out a gray metal box and opens it. After some rustling, he pulls out two photographs.

"Here," he says, handing them to me.

One is of a black and white portrait of Mr. Johnson, his ex-wife Lois, and what looks like a newborn. I flip over the photograph. Written in the upper right hand corner is, "The Johnson Family — Cleotis, Lois, and Dexter." The second photo is the one Mrs. Winston has in the pocket watch — Mr. Johnson holding Dexter.

"His mama was something. Potts and Winston tried to tell me that she was no good, but I couldn't hear them."

He takes the photos and puts them back in the box.

"That woman took my son and ran off with some fool named Roscoe. If I coulda just got my hands on him. He lucky they killed him before I got to him."

"She didn't let you see him at all?"

"After things died down a little, she would let me see him, but I could tell the environment was no good for him. Her and that man was teaching him some ugly stuff. Them two had a baby together too."

"Richard."

"Yep. Dexter — I like to call him Dexter when I ain't around church folks — loved his little brother. I used to take them both out when Lois would let me. But as they got older, they changed. Just got mean. Everything was about money and what they could get. Dexter stopped calling me 'Daddy.' Called me 'Johnson,' among other nasty names. We had one final and terrible fight and he took his step daddy's last name — Tremmel."

"Did you ever hit him?"

"I'm getting' to that boy. Well — yeah. That changed our relationship. But I had to defend myself. He was in his early teens and, believe or not, he came to visit me while I was on a trip to New York. I caught him taking money out of my wallet, so I yelled at him. Told him to put it back. He said, "Go to hell, old man. I do what I damn well please. You ain't nobody to be tellin' me what to do." Then he pushed me. I said to myself, if he wants to act like a man, I'm going to treat him like one." I reached back and slapped the shit out of him. Knocked him over the table. I could tell he was shocked, but then he pulled a knife. My own son pulled a knife on me. And the look in his eyes was that he meant to hurt me. I grabbed my jacket, wrapped it around my left arm to protect myself. He lunged at me, and I moved out of the way. He lost his balance, and I caught him in the jaw with my right hand, just hard enough to stop him. When he fell, the knife slid under the couch. He was crying, and so was I. I tried to comfort him, but he snatched away.

"'I'ma get you. I'ma get you.' That's what he said when he ran out of my room."

"Wow. Was he hurt?"

"No. Busted lip. But his pride was hurt. He was embarrassed."

"What happened after that?"

"Well, I had to hear his mama's mouth. I told her what he did, but she made it my fault."

"Did you see him again?"

"Yeah, but I shouldn't have."

"What do you mean?"

"He called me while he was in college and said he wanted to see me. I said okay because — that's my son — no matter what — he'll always be my son."

Mr. Johnson's eyes start to well. His voice shakes.

"I went to Maryland. Stayed at his apartment. I thought we was reconciling, but he was settin' me up."

"Huh? How?"

"The second or third night I was there, he took me out to hear some live jazz. The last thing I remember is waking up the next morning at his apartment, and him screaming at me.

"'Get yo' ass up old man. I want you to see this.'"

I didn't know what was going on. Why was he talking to me like this? Then, he drug me in the living room. There were pictures everywhere of me with little boys, children. Son, I would never do anything to hurt a child, but he and his brother made it look so real. I almost believed myself."

"Why did you do this?" I asked.

"I told you I was gonna get you. Now here's the deal. Soon, I'm coming to Grimmel. I've got plans for that place.

You're gonna take yo' ass back there and keep yo' mouth shut. These pictures? They are my insurance policy. You even act like you want to say something about me or whatever I do, I'll show these to everybody."

"Why are you doing this, Dexter?"

"Shut up, you ol' fool. Don't say nothin' else. You know my 'other daddy,' in between beatin' my mother, brother, and me, taught me well. I got you. Now pack yo' shit and get back to Grimmel. By the way, my mother told me about Flora Potts and Emma Winston. Be sure to tell them I won't hesitate killing them or anybody close to them if they utter a word.

"Tremmel is a calculating, cunning bastard. You remember when he and Ms. Sonya got here?"

"Yes, sir."

"Lord, that poor lady. He had them people in Grimmel and Mt. Sinai fooled. People thought I didn't like him because I wanted to be in charge. I ain't care nothing about bein' in charge. I just didn't wanna see people taken advantage of. Yeah, Tremmel did some good stuff to keep them fooled, but they didn't see how he treated his wife when the spotlight wasn't on him.

"I didn't trust Tremmel from the beginning 'cause I knew him. The only reason I stayed at Sinai was to keep an eye on that slick rascal."

Mr. Johnson was always watching him. Now I understood why.

"Sometimes he didn't know I was close enough to hear him, but some of the stuff he would say to that woman was terrible. Heard him call her a 'bitch' right there on the church ground.

"They was in his office one time, and he told her she wasn't no count — wasn't worth the dog shit he scraped of the bottom of his shoe. Told her she was gettin' fat and needed to stop eatin' so much. Said nobody was gonna want her fat ass."

"Really? He said that to her?"

"If I'm lyin' I'm flyin.' Shit. I ain't got nothin' to lose. Yeah, he's, he's my — son. But he don't pay a thing for me. If he treats his wife like that, how do you think he gon' treat the church and the people in it? Hell, look at what he's done to me? He treated that lady one way in front of folks, and I think he do the same thing with the church."

"Wow."

"Wow is right. People just see what they wanna see. He's mana— manip —

"Manipulative?"

"Yeah. He got Percy, Lawrence and Preston in his back pocket. And he makes the trustees do whatever he say. But everything looks different to the congregation. If I call him on his bullshit, I look like the mean old man."

Did Mr. Johnson say "shit" twice? He's really upset.

"Excuse my French son, but that's what it is — bullshit."

"It's okay, Mr. Johnson. I understand. Sometimes you got to call a spade a spade."

"That's right boy. That's right."

He sits down on a straight back chair and puts his snuff cup on the edge of the table, but he only gets part of it, and it's about to fall.

I'm not moving to catch that.

"Mr. Johnson. Your cup." I yell.

"What?"

He turns just in time to catch it before it hits the floor.

"Thank you son. That woulda been a mess."

I look at the rug and see that he didn't catch his cups too often.

"Mason, I'm getting old. Too old to keep up with Tremmel. I know he's my blood, but I'm tired. Sometimes I forget that he's a part of me. But he's so mean, hateful. He needs to go. Sometimes I wish he were — God help me — dead. And now there's two of 'em. And that Richard is nickel slick. I can't do it no mo'. I want you to watch 'em, Mason. Please keep an eye on 'em. There's too many good peoples at that church."

"Yes, sir, Mr. Johnson. I'll watch him."

"Son, I ain't said this to nobody, but I have a feeling he had something to do with Ms. Sonya dying."

Me too.

"You want something to eat, Mason? I got plenty."

I look at that cup. Smell the boiled chicken stench.

"No thank you, Mr. Johnson. But I appreciate the offer."

"Okay. You don't know what you missing."

Yes, I do.

"I gotta go. Thanks again."

I close the door behind me, leaving him with the boiled chicken and tobacco juice.

That was the last time I saw Mr. Johnson. He had a stroke two days later and never left the hospital.

CHAPTER NINETEEN

"Mason, telephone. It's Rhonda." my sister yells. She sticks her tongue out at me, hands me the phone and runs out to the back door to play.

Wow. It's early for her to call on a Saturday.

"Good morning. This is early for you isn't it?" I ask.

There's silence.

"Hello? Rhonda? Are you there?"

"Yes, but I have some news. Tremmel's dead"

"What? Dead? Rev. Tremmel's dead?"

"Yes, he is."

"What happened?"

"I don't know yet. Someone just called my mom. I'll let you know when I hear anything else."

"Okay. I'm sure we'll be getting phone calls any minute. I'll call you back in a little while."

Watching my mother's face when I told her about Rev. Tremmel was heart breaking.

"What happened?" she asked.

"I don't know. Rhonda said that — "

R-r-ring. R-r-ring.

And the phone calls start.

After my mother hangs up, I ask her if she has any news on what happened.

"They're not sure," she says.

"When Mr. Sweets was cleaning up the church this morning, he found him layin' face down on the floor in his study."

I don't know what to think, say, or do. Both Tremmel and Ms. Sonya? Did he have a heart attack? Stroke?

My parents began to theorize about what might have possibly happened. The phone rings incessantly.

I walk outside and sit on the edge of the porch. It's late May. A beautiful spring day.

This is unbelievable. Rev. Tremmel dead? How? Why? What happened? I look toward the slightly overcast sky framed by the maple tree's branches. I look to my right and see two of my sisters preparing to ride their bikes. They don't have a clue about what's happened and don't need to know anything at this point.

I look to my left and see Dep walking up the sidewalk toward me. When I see his face, I know he knows.

"You heard what happened, right?" I ask.

"Yeah."

"You know what happened?"

"Naw. They ain't sure. My mama said something about a heart attack, but they don't know.

You know Mr. Sweets that cleans the church?"

"Yeah, I know him. I heard he found him."

"Yeah, he's the one that found him. He told my mama it was a mess. From what he could tell, she said, somebody put a whoopin' on him and killed him. "

Dep steps up on the porch and sits in the peeling brown wicker chair. We sit there for a long time, communicating, but not saying a word.

The reports start to come in. Somebody stabbed Tremmel to death with a writing pen.

"Yes, child," we heard my mother on the phone. "Somebody stabbed him in the neck with one of them expensive writing pens. A Wispy Adipinch or something like."

Wasp Addipoint. Oh my goodness. That was my pen. That's the one Rhonda gave me. Tremmel never brings his to church, and I let him borrow mine a few weeks ago for some special letters he said he had to write. I saw it sitting on his desk this past Sunday. Nobody knew he borrowed it but me.

But stabbed to death with that? Who? Why?

***

After a couple of weeks, this is still a mystery. No one has seen Richard. Church services are cancelled until further notice.

I start to think hard about this. The police have no clues. No fingerprints. No motive. Nothing.

Who would want to kill Tremmel bad enough to do this? No one in the congregation knows what I know. Mr. Johnson is dead. Neither Mrs. Potts nor Mrs. Winston could do this. They're not strong enough. The official report is that the murder was extremely violent and forceful. Rhonda and I were together at the time it happened, and Ms. Franks was with us.

Where were my boys at that time? I'm starting to get nervous. I know they hated him after I told them what he was doing to Ms. Sonya, Ms. Franks, and Rhonda. But to kill him? Did they hate him enough to kill him?

We better talk. Maybe they know something. I'm supposed to meet Rhonda in an hour. I call and postpone.

"Is everything okay?" she asks.

"I think so. I've got to check on something. I'll talk to you later.

The guys come by my house and we meet in my room. We shoot the breeze for a few minutes — graduation, parties, school.

Finally, I put my fingers to my lips to signal them to be quiet. I crack my door. No one is within earshot.

I whisper, "What did you guys do?

"What are you talking about? Dep asks.

"What do you mean?"

"Did you guys take out Tremmel?"

Silence. No eye contact.

"Come on guys. What's going on?

More silence.

"I know you did it or you know something. What happened?"

"Whatever we say, it's under the pact. Right?" Link asks.

"Right," I say.

CHAPTER TWENTY

Link whispers. "I took him out. Yes, I killed Rev. Tremmel."

There's silence. I look at the floor. I look at the guys. Their faces have no expression. I don't know what I'm feeling.

"Why?" I ask. "Why'd you do that?"

"I know about what my grandmother told you. I talked to Ms. Franks too. It was time for him to go down. The police weren't gonna do nothing. Butterfield? That fat redneck was so far up Tremmel's butt he could smell his breath."

Link has a black bag on his shoulder. He takes it off and places it carefully on the floor.

"Tremmel and Richard had them clowns eating out of the palm of his hand. Remember that mess with BJ? I cornered him one day after school, and he told me that Tremmel and some guy he didn't know messed him up, and said that if he bothered us again they'd kill him. Tremmel was untouchable. He had to die."

"But Dep was here right after — "

"Yeah we know."

"He swore he wouldn't tell and he didn't. He was under the pact with us."

"So what happened? How'd you do it?"

"This is how it went down."

***

Around 11:30 p.m., Link called Tremmel with the excuse that he got himself in trouble with some girl. He thinks she's pregnant and needs to talk. He asked Tremmel if he would meet him at the church so they could talk face to face. Tremmel agreed.

Dep slipped in Tremmel's study through a window that's always unlocked and opened the door so Link could come in. Link hid in the closet and Dep behind the bookcase. Mitchell and Marshall stood guard outside.

They all wore black gloves and ski masks. Link armed himself with a hookbill blade. Dep planned to use his fists.

Tremmel came in and turned on the desk lamp. He bent down to pick up spilled pencils on the floor Dep had strategically knocked over. When Tremmel bent down, Link leaped out of the closet onto Tremmel's back and cut him deep in his left shoulder. Tremmel stood up but Link hung on. Tremmel rammed himself backward into the wall, causing Link to drop the knife, but he still held on to Tremmel's neck.

Tremmel flipped Link on the ground. But Dep came from behind the bookcase and grabbed Tremmel's legs tight so he couldn't move them. Link jumped up quickly, dodged a right cross from Tremmel. And he ran straight at Tremmel's chest, knocking him backwards on the desk.

Link jumped on top of Tremmel, but he grabbed Link's throat hard and tight with both hands. Link could feel the breath leaving his body, and he couldn't inhale. Dep moved from Tremmel's legs and pummeled his face repeatedly, but he wouldn't let go of Link's neck.

Link swung wildly and pulled at Tremmel's hands and arms. Out of the corner of his right eye he saw the calligraphy pen on the corner of the desk. With all his might he stretched his right hand to reach it, but Tremmel squeezed his throat harder and harder. Link pulled at Tremmel's hands, but they had his neck locked.

Link summoned all his strength and could finally touch the top of the pen with his fingertips. He nudged it toward him, as he fought to keep from losing consciousness. He kept pushing and moving the pen until he could grab it, and slammed it into Tremmel's throat, — straight through the trachea.

Tremmel gasped and gagged when Link opened the hole in his throat.

Link quickly pulled the pen out and thrust it into Tremmel's left carotid artery. Tremmel let go of Link's neck and grabbed his own. Blood squirted through his fingers, splattered on the wall, and sprayed the carpet. Dep jumped backed to avoid the blood, but kept striking Tremmel's head.

Dep said that Link jumped on top of him, straddling his chest, while Tremmel grabbed his neck and throat — gurgling and gasping, kicking and flailing. As he struggled to breathe his last, Link stared into Tremmel's eyes and slowly removed his mask.

"That's right you dirty son of a bitch. I want you to see me. You killed my father, Daniel. Daniel Lane. Remember him? I want you to see his son's face as he takes your life from you, bitch. This is also for Ms. Sonya. Yeah, we know what you did. Go to hell, Tremmel."

Tremmel's eyes were wide with disbelief that Link exposed his secrets to his face. Blood poured from the left side of his neck. Faint gurgles percolated in the back of his throat.

Tremmel stopped moving. His eyes stared up blankly at Link's face.

Marshall called from outside the window, "What's happening?"

"It's done," Link said, as he climbed off Tremmel's bleeding body and spit on his bruised face.

"Open the door then," Mitchell said.

Dep went out of the study and let Mitchell and Marshall inside. They wiped down the pen and the entire room, made sure that there were no prints, grabbed got the knife, and got out of there. Their clothes became ashes. The knife is on the bottom of the Jason River.

***

"That's what happened," Link says. "I wished his punk ass brother Richard was there. He would've gotten the same thing. Ain't nobody seen him. He did the right thing in getting out of Grimmel."

The rest of them nod in agreement.

"Are you guys okay?" I ask. "Damn. I can't believe you killed this guy."

"Yeah, we did. Well, I did." Link says. "Yep, I killed him. That piece of shit killed my father, man, and Ms. Sonya. He's been torturing people, beating women, and getting away with all of it for a long time.

"I know what the Bible says and all that. But I did this. I know what I did. I'll deal with it when and if I have to. But for now, that cat is history.

"By the way, thanks for telling me where the film and negatives were. We got those too."

Link reaches in the bag he had on his shoulder and pulls out a smaller black bag filled with 16 mm film and 35 mm negatives.

"Here you go."

"Thanks. Hey did you get my fifty bucks from him?"

We crack up laughing. It eases the tension.

Once we gather ourselves, I move to the middle of the room.

"I have something to say fellas. I know guys aren't supposed to say this, but I have to.

I exhale.

"I don't know what to think about what you did, but it's done. Somebody was bound to do it. But enough about that."

I exhale again.

"I love you guys. You know our lives won't ever be the same after this summer. I don't know what's going to happen to us, but I want all of you guys to know that — I love you."

For a few seconds, there's silence. They're all looking down not sure what to do. Then Link walks over to me, shakes my hand and gives me a big hug.

"I love you too, man," he says with a grin.

Link's actions break the spell and give everyone permission to move. Handshakes, hugs, misty eyes, and sniffles all around.

The love my friends, my brothers and I share is genuine, mutual and eternal.

Before we depart, we affirm under the pact to never speak of the Tremmel incident again.

"It never happened," Dep says. "It's wiped from our minds for good."

We nod in agreement.

Everyone leaves. I pour myself a cool glass of water and have a seat on the edge of the porch. The night is still. Stars are everywhere. They're beautiful. But it feels like they're looking down and beckoning me. It's like the universe has been waiting for me to step outside so it can help me process what's happened.

I spend most of the night meditating on what my boys did and what they told me. I know that Link has taken a life, and I can't lie. It bothers me. But honestly, part of me feels a great sense of relief.

But still, a man is dead. Even though he was garbage in the eyes of many, he was a mother's son, a brother, and a leader for others. Was Link right to take his life? I don't know. I know what the Bible says, the law and all of that, but is there a time when something like this should happen? Isn't the world better off with someone like him gone? Maybe. What would I do if someone killed my father? What if they beat and did unspeakable things to my mother? I honestly don't know what I would do. It's easy to say what I think I would do, but I wouldn't know unless it happened to me and the time came to make a decision.

I exhale and do my best to let it go.

The next day, Rhonda and I have lunch at the drugstore and talk about what happened to Tremmel. I can't tell her how it went down, but she feels the same way I do and shares some of the same struggles.

"I don't want to see anyone murdered, but I can't say I feel sad for him. Actually, I'm relieved. I don't know if I could have killed him, but I'm glad that he's not going to bother us or anybody else anymore.

"Nobody knows where Richard is, huh?" she asks.

"No. I haven't heard anything."

I'm pretty hungry, so I finish my burger and fries quickly. But it hits the spot.

"I'm full Mason. Do you want my fries?"

"No thanks. I'm full too. I'll get a takeout box for you."

The clerk hands me a small paper box, and she puts half of her chicken salad sandwich and fries inside.

"Don't forget to put that in the fridge as soon as you get home," I say.

She smiles. "I won't. And thanks for lunch."

"It was my pleasure."

There's something I've been meaning to ask Rhonda since I talked to Mrs. Potts, but I don't know if I should. I decide to fish before we leave.

"I know you didn't know your dad, but what has your mother told you about him?"

She looks up and to the left, trying to recall the information. "Well, he was handsome. Smart. Goal oriented, A little eccentric. A very good man."

"And what happened to him?"

"Mason, I know." She gazes at my eyes.

"What do you mean, you know?"

"I know what happened to him. My mother told me after she told you to talk to Mrs. Potts. I know Tremmel murdered my father."

"Whew."

"What?"

"I'm so glad. When Mrs. Potts told me, I wanted to tell you, but it wasn't my place. I still thought you should know, but I wasn't sure how or what to do."

She smiles.

"That's what I love about you. You're always taking care of somebody. I'm glad you're looking out for me."

"Always."

"We need to talk to your mother."

"Okay. Let's go."

When we get to her house, we find Ms. Franks watching television. She looks relaxed.

"Hey, Ms. Franks. How are you?"

"Well hello, Mason. I'm fine. It's good to see you."

"Ms. Franks, I hate to interrupt your show, but I have something to show you. Do you mind?"

"Really? Do I want to see it?

"I think you do, Mama," Rhonda says.

I show the bag of film and negatives to Ms. Franks. The tears in her eyes and the smile that appears on her face are beyond words. She's grateful, but refuses to touch them.

"How did you — Where did — Forget it. I don't even want to know. Mason, Thank you so much."

She gives me the biggest and tightest hug.

"You don't know how much this means. Oh my goodness. I'm free."

Her hands cover her face as she sobs joyfully. She eventually gathers herself.

"But I don't want to touch that filth. Mason, you and Rhonda please get rid of those for me. Please."

"Yes, ma'am."

Rhonda and I take a walk in the woods behind her house. I find a flat rock and use it to dig a hole and toss in the film and negatives. Rhonda douses them with lighter fluid she brought from their garage. With the strike of one match, Ms. Franks and others are out of bondage.

Rhonda and I embrace and watch the string of smoke from the burning celluloid rise slowly above the trees.

Graduation finally arrives. It's a typical boring ceremony. Mayor Adams is the keynote. Between campaigning and pontificating, he does a wonderful job annoying folks and putting others to sleep. If it wasn't for the excitement of this being the last night I'll be a high school student, I'd be out like a light too.

"Thank you, Mayor Adams." Principal Lane says. Faint applause accompanies him to his seat on the rostrum.

That's the cue for the moment I dreamed about from the first bus ride of the school year to now — the call of graduates' names. I'm one of the first.

As I walk across the stage I hear my family cheering. My boys are shouting, "Mason, Mason." I relish this moment.

I get back to my seat and join everyone in cheering for Rhonda and the rest of the guys as they strut to get their diplomas and shake Principal Lane and the other dignitaries' hands.

After the class recesses, we gather in the lobby, pose for pictures with each other and our families.

I find a moment to myself in a corridor where the administrative offices are located. I look at my diploma and read it silently, carefully, and proudly.

> Grimmel High School certifies that Mason L. Alexander having satisfactorily completed the course of studies prescribed by the Board of Education of Yellowstone County and is entitled to this diploma.

High School is done.

"Congratulations Mason." my sisters yell.

"Come in the kitchen. We have something for you."

My baby sister is dancing around like she graduated. Oh wow. There's a cake. That's why she's dancing. It says in bold baby blue letters, "Well Done Mason. Congratulations."

"Thank you guys." I say.

"You done good big head." another sister says.

We feast on cake and punch for awhile.

"Come here son," my father says. He puts his arm around me and we walk out on the front porch.

"Son, I'm proud of you. You done everythin' we asked — and — "

He chokes up for second.

"You've made us proud. You're a man today. I believe you can do anything you want. Don't let nobody tell you that you can't."

He forces an envelope in my hand.

"Here's a little something from your mother and me. Take it and have some fun. We love you son."

He pats me on the shoulder and goes back inside. My mother's standing in the doorway watching us. Tears run down her face. She smiles.

"You goin' to stay out here a little while?" she asks.

"Yes, ma'am. Just for a little while."

"Okay."

I take a sip of punch and nestle in the brown wicker chair.

Memories of our summer lying fests race through my mind. The hours of basketball, heartbreaks, death, and life engulf me and remind me of how I've reached this point. My boys, Marshall, Mitchell, Dep and Link — and now Rhonda — people besides my family I would give my life for. What's going to become of us?

***

Wow. I didn't realize I've been out here for over two hours. It's quiet. I walk through the house. My sisters are asleep in their room. The opened window provides a gateway for a gentle breeze that comforts them in their slumber. They've had a great time tonight. It's evident in my baby sister who's in bed with my older sister. She's curled under her chin and clutching a ratty pink stuffed bunny under her arm. That bunny has seen better days, but he's been with her since she was born. In her opposite hand she holds a cherry lollipop stolen from the bowl on the kitchen table. I'm surprised it's not stuck to the sheet. Her slightly opened lips are blue and purple from the cake's icing. I take a picture with my mind's eye of all of them and slide the lollipop from her fingers.

"Sleep tight y'all."

My parents are in their room. I don't hear the television, so I'm sure they're asleep too.

Nights like this will be over soon, so I wrap this one carefully and put it in a safe place.

***

As the summer draws to a close and we all prepare for the next phase of life, I learn that my man Marshall's going to continue in the family bakery business. Marshall couldn't wait to get out of school, and I'm so proud he didn't quit.

I can't believe he's dating Cheryl. I knew something was up. He hemmed and hawed when I asked him about her. Sly rascal.

Cheryl's even cooler than I thought, and I can tell that Marshall really likes her.

Marshall and Fast Cheryl. Wow.

Mitchell never really talked about college. But oh how things change. He starts Trane Community College in a few weeks. He's talking about becoming a lawyer, and has enrolled in the paralegal program.

When I think about it, that fits Mitchell. Anybody that can lie as good as he should make an excellent lawyer.

Dep's always been street smart and a good student. The guy can do anything, and has the tenacity to succeed no matter the odds. He's leaving Grimmel and heading to Alabama A&T.

Dep and I used to practice Spanish and French. We were both tops in our classes, but I forgot how good that country boy is at languages. He's going to be majoring in International Banking. Spain better look out. Alabama A&T is throwing money at him to keep him from going any place else.

Link's going to Florida Central College to study Communications. Link is another guy that keeps his talents quiet. He jokes me about my love of the arts, but he's an incredible writer. He's written a ton of short stories ranging from love, race, to science fiction. Link writes so well. He's already has a couple of pieces ready for publication.

He and I vow to collaborate on something. We don't know what it is yet, but I know it'll happen. Link is the epitome of a true friend. A best friend.

Rhonda will be a student at Georgia State studying English. She wants to be a college professor. I know that she can do anything she wants. I want to be by her side when she does it.

I decide Maryland State University isn't for me. Some of it has to do with the Tremmel deal, but I just don't want to go there anymore.

I'll be at the University of Georgia studying Art. I'm going to be an illustrator. One day I'll illustrate books that I write.

We decide to meet at the bus station to see Dep off for Alabama. He's the first of us boys to leave.

As the bus driver loads Dep's bags in the compartment, I hold Rhonda's hand and look around one more time at my friends.

I wouldn't trade a thing for my experiences with them.

The driver revs the engine. The last passengers make their way onboard.

Dep peers at us through the window. He makes faces to ease the tension and sadness of his departure. We smile and wave.

The bus pulls slowly out of the station, turns left down Main St, and eventually disappears over the horizon.

We feel the change coming and prepare for the next chapter of our lives.

CPSIA information can be obtained
at www.ICGtesting.com
Printed in the USA
FFOW02n1618270517
35973FF